I0740132

Simply Irresistible

Simply Irresistible

A Spruce Creek Romance

SHARON BURGESS

A Russian Hill Press Book
United States • United Kingdom • Australia

Russian Hill Press
The publisher is not responsible for websites (or their content)
that are not owned by the publisher.

Cover Design: Christine McCall
Cover Photograph: Guenter M. Kirchweger
Cover Silhouette: Craig Toron
Editor: Kristi Cook

LCCN: 2014939844
ISBN: 978-0-9911973-9-2

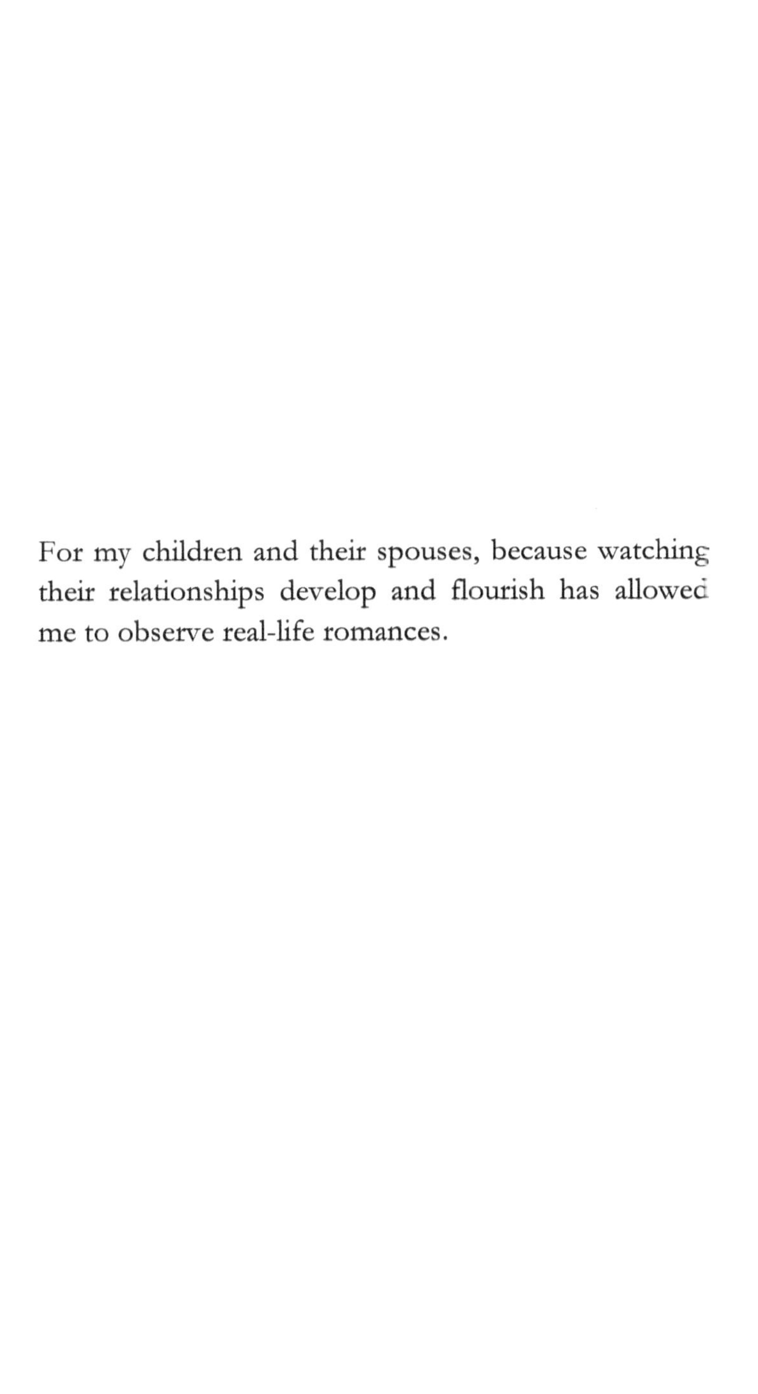

For my children and their spouses, because watching their relationships develop and flourish has allowed me to observe real-life romances.

ACKNOWLEDGMENTS

Special thanks to my critique partners, Judy and Nate; to my beta readers, Anne and Julie; to all my supporters in the California Writers Club and at the San Francisco Area Chapter, Romance Writers of America; and finally, saving the best until last, everlasting gratitude to my incredible editor, Kristi Cook.

Without all of you this book would never have made it into print.

ONE

J ordan Walker, DVM, grimaced at the cacophony of chaotic sounds coming from his reception area—barking dogs, shouting voices, clanging telephones. The barking wasn't unusual, but normally his employees and the pet owners didn't shout at each other.

Jordan had just finished a difficult surgery, the last of the day. He was tired, his scrubs were soiled with blood and hair, and his tolerance was fleeing. Since he was not fit to be seen by man or animal, he had every intention of turning a deaf ear to whatever was happening. He started to retreat further from the front office area, when the door to reception opened and Torrey Hansen, his office manager, hailed him. "Doctor, we need you in the front, right now. Mr. Gardner has a problem with his bill."

"Well, take care of his problem," Jordan retorted, gritting his teeth to restrain his frustration. "That's *your* responsibility—I just do the dirty work around here."

"You don't understand," Torrey contended, "he claims he can't afford to pay such an outrageous amount—his words, not mine—but he insists on taking his cat, Clementine, home with him today. Since it's *your* policy that pets can't be released until the bill is paid, you need to deal with this."

Harnessing his diminishing patience, Jordan walked through another door, directly into the cat waiting area. The Cat Pit, as it was named, was separated from the Dog Pound by the horseshoe-shaped counter behind which the front office staff worked. He barely glanced toward the three canines that were being ineffectively shushed by their owners.

Old man Gardner, aged and white-haired, wore faded khakis and a much-washed red flannel shirt. The shirt hung on his spare frame, causing Jordan to think of the scarecrow in *The Wizard of Oz.*

Waving a piece of paper, Gardner rushed Jordan as he entered. "I can't afford to pay this—

this outrageous bill," he sputtered. "Your father never charged rates like this, and he wouldn't hold Clementine hostage for payment, either. You may be an excellent vet, but you aren't half the human being your father was."

Jordan wondered why he stayed in private practice—certainly there were fewer headaches and more money to be made working in government or research. He felt his irritation level escalating. He was going to lose his temper and yell at a senior citizen—just what his image needed.

"Mr. Gardner," he replied, holding himself tightly in check, "while it's true that, when I took over my father's practice, I altered rates and policies, these actions were required to cover my overhead and stay in business." *Why did he even feel it necessary to justify himself to this old man?*

Before Jordan could continue his lecture, a staff member he didn't recognize interrupted him. True, his office manager, Torrey, did most of the hiring and firing, but this young woman didn't look old enough to be a veterinary assistant. She was petite, barely reaching the middle of his chest. Her russet hair was bound in two braids— pigtails, he thought they were called. Freckles dotted her nose, and she wore a yellow smock decorated with puppies and kittens.

"Doctor, I think you're needed in surgery," she said, touching his hand as if to get his attention. "If I may, I'll assist Mr. Gardner. I think we might have failed to apply the senior discount, which is why the bill is so high."

Senior discount? Jordan disregarded the spark that surged through him at the touch of her hand. *I haven't approved any senior discount. But hey, if this little Heidi character thinks she can bring peace and quiet to the clinic, I'll let her try.*

Jordan retreated through the door to the rear, his temper simmering but his dignity intact. Peering through a crack, he watched the new veterinary assistant take Mr. Gardner gently by the hand and lead him back to the seating area.

"You wait here, and I'll bring Clementine to you," she said. "I'll ask the cashier to recalculate your charges after applying the senior discount. If the bill is still too high for you to pay at once, we'll arrange a payment plan. You won't need to worry about that today—you can take Clementine home and we'll mail you the bill."

Jordan continued to spy through the door while this unknown employee demolished all his established fiscal practices, one by one.

"I thought young Dr. Walker didn't approve

of payment plans," Gardner retorted. "He's a cold-hearted bastard—pardon my language, Miss—but he makes me angry."

"He *did* manage to heal Clementine for you, and she was seriously ill. So he can't be all rotten, can he?" she asked, squeezing his hand. "Just wait here and I'll be right back."

After Gardner and Clementine had departed the clinic, Jordan poked his head into the staff area and asked Torrey to join him in the back.

"Who is this little Heidi look-alike who intervened between Gardner and me?" he asked as soon as she appeared. "I don't recall having seen her before. How long has she been working here?"

"Her name is Kathleen Morelli—Kat to her colleagues. She's been with us just over a week. She's a sweet girl."

"Are you certain she's legally old enough to work?"

"Of course she is," Torrey answered with a laugh. "She has excellent credentials. She graduated from State with an AVMA approved degree as a veterinary technician. She has NAVTA certification, and she worked for Jim Foley in Ft. Collins before she came here. You just haven't met her yet because you were gone all last week. Don't worry, I'll introduce you."

"That might be a smart idea since I *am* paying her salary. Give me time to clean up, then bring her to my office."

A few minutes later, Torrey introduced Kat to Jordan, who sat stiffly erect behind his desk, doing his best to look uncompromising. His space was designed to enforce a feeling of intimidation. The oversize desk was mahogany. A matching credenza behind him held his computer. Large, heavy bookcases stood across from the desk, and two uncomfortable visitor chairs rested in front of the bookcases.

Jordan had washed up, sprinkled on some cologne, combed his hair, and disposed of the surgical bonnet and booties he'd been wearing when he rushed into the waiting area. In a clean lab coat, he knew he looked the part of a successful medical professional.

When Kat was seated in the chair in front of him, Jordan looked at her for the first time—really looked. He found himself sinking into her deep blue eyes. They were like gemstones, the color of a glacier lake, and he was spellbound. He couldn't remember ever having seen eyes that color blue.

"Well, Ms. Morelli, that was a timely

intervention you made," he said abruptly. "However, I'm not certain how you think we should resolve the problem. You *are* aware, are you not, that I don't have a senior discount policy at this clinic?"

"Well, you should have." She straightened her back and glared—a force five tornado assaulting Mount Rushmore. "Old people living on pensions can't afford high prices. Frequently, their pets are the only family they have, the only ones who care about them. Sometimes seniors are forced to choose between feeding themselves and taking care of their animals."

"And this should concern me . . . why?" Jordan's voice dripped with sarcasm.

He saw a look of disgust on her face. His attitude had shocked her. He wasn't certain why he cared, but suddenly he didn't want this pert young woman to think badly of him. Maybe he'd see what arrangements could be made to reduce Mr. Gardner's bill. He would also ask Torrey if the clinic now could provide some sort of ongoing senior discount policy. The clinic had moved financially into the black, after all.

"I'll consider your suggestions, Ms. Morelli," he replied, hiding a smile. "You do surprise me, however. You are a brand new employee and yet you contest my policies. Torrey is the only person working here who's ever had the nerve to lecture me. I hope this won't become a habit."

He stood to indicate the interview was at an end and ushered her out the door.

KAT SEETHED, READY TO EXPLODE, as she walked away from Jordan Walker's office. Her boss could only be described as cold and callous. He was a pompous ass.

She didn't like the man, but she would tolerate him. She had to. She had bills and student loans and rent and car payments. If she quit or was fired, her parents would point out what a disappointment she was and ask why she couldn't do things right—like her brother.

Stiffening her spine, she decided she had no intention of leaving Spruce Creek. The quaint Colorado mountain town was her home now. The century-old buildings—and newer ones constructed to look as if they were—housed a community nestled in a small park-like setting bisected by its namesake. A single-lane bridge spanned the creek, allowing only one vehicle at a time to cross.

In just a short time, Kat had come to love the

small town, the people who lived there, and her job working with animals. Since she planned to stay, she would just have to refashion Jordan Walker into a sensitive human being. She had her work cut out for her.

Kat rushed to find Torrey, the office manager, to discuss what she should do about the confrontation. But she found, instead, that Torrey had left for the day, as had the rest of the front office personnel. The doors were locked, and the reception and exam room lights were off.

Damn! The conversation she desperately wanted to have right this minute must wait until tomorrow.

She stomped into the staff room, pulled on her jacket, and furious, grabbed her bag before turning to leave by the back exit. Since there were no windows in the rear portion of the animal hospital, none of the waning daylight from the sinking sun intruded into the work area.

A few animals were settled quietly in their boarding cages. The smell of warm bodies permeated the air. The clinic was kept scrupulously clean, so there was no smell of urine or feces.

Had she not been so angry she might have noticed sooner that there was something . . . off.

Something strange—an unfamiliar scent, spicy and peculiar.

The cleaning crew hadn't yet arrived and she was alone. She felt spooked—a shiver ran down her spine. Her anger was replaced by a sense of foreboding. *Was the back door open?*

All the lights were muted or turned off for the night. The chill intensified. Goose bumps rose on her arms. She forced herself through the darkened clinic toward the pharmacy, where a light burned. She walked forward calling out, "Dr. Walker, are you here? Is anyone here?"

Kat heard no response and stuck her head in through the door. She sensed a presence in the room. Suddenly the light went out and, without warning, pain stabbed into her temple. She was shoved off her feet, and her head struck the door jamb.

When she regained consciousness, panic consumed her—heart racing, breath laboring, palms sweating. She didn't know where she was or what had happened. She only knew she had a piercing headache and the bitter taste of blood in her mouth.

After her racing heart slowed, Kat looked around. She saw the open pharmacy door and realized she'd been attacked. Pulling her cell phone from the bag lying next to her, she dialed nine-one-one. In spite of a crushing headache, she managed to tell the dispatcher what had happened, instructing that the emergency personnel should enter through the back.

Sirens blaring and lights flashing, the deputies arrived in record time considering the eleven miles of mountain highway they'd driven from Bailey.

She heard a voice at the same time she saw a flashlight glow. "Park County Sheriff, is anybody here?"

Weakly, she called out, "Here—I'm here. I'm hurt."

The beam of light found her and the officer called out loudly "Clear" to the paramedics waiting impatiently until the area was secured.

"Where are you hurt?" an EMT asked as he wrapped Kat's arm in a blood pressure cuff. "Relax if you can, we're here to help you."

The overhead lights flared on as Jordan Walker came through the door. "What's going on here?" he yelled.

"Who are you?" a deputy yelled back while reaching for his weapon.

"Stop, please," Kat whimpered. She hated feeling vulnerable.

Spotting Kat behind the paramedics, Jordan hurried to her side. "Kat, uh—Ms. Morelli—what happened? Are you okay?"

Both a paramedic and a deputy stepped forward to restrain him.

"It's okay," she told them. "He's Dr. Walker. He owns this clinic."

A detective strode through the back door just as she called off her two would-be protectors. He waved the deputy away. "Dr. Walker, I'm Detective Turner. Can you tell me what happened?"

"I don't know, I just got here," he replied. "We need to ask Ms. Morelli. She's the one who's injured."

Turner looked at Jordan. "And how did you get here so fast?"

"I live upstairs, in an apartment over the clinic. I heard the sirens and saw the lights, and I came down as soon as I could get shoes on."

Turner looked to the paramedics. "Can I ask her a few questions?"

The paramedics turned to Kat. "Do you feel up to answering questions? They can wait until you get to the treatment center, if you want."

"Now's fine," she said. She told them the short version, about the lights being out and checking the premises before leaving for the night. How she was surprised to find the pharmacy open and a light on. How she stuck her head in to check and then it was lights out, literally.

Kat watched Turner accompany Jordan into the pharmacy to see what had been taken. The steel cabinets which held the narcotics were still secure. She could tell that Jordan was concerned to find that the drawer holding tranquilizer darts had been broken into. She listened as Turner asked the implications of their use against a human.

"Since I primarily treat small animals—cats and dogs—in the clinic, the darts I keep on-hand here are low dosage. They might affect an adult, but not much. They would be more effective against a small child.

"How about if more than one were used on an adult?" Turner asked.

"That might be problematic," Jordan replied. Then he rushed away, calling behind him, "I need to check the garage. I keep stronger darts in my truck in case I'm called out on a lion sighting at the campground."

When he returned, apparently satisfied that the garage was secure, he approached the EMT who was treating Kat.

"I only have a headache," she claimed. "I'm going to live. I don't need to go to the ER."

Before the paramedic could respond, Jordan spoke up. "Kat—uh, Ms. Morelli," he corrected. "You *are* going to the emergency room. You might have a concussion. In fact, that's a probability. As your boss and as a doctor, I am not allowing you to do anything else." He spoke emphatically—his words were steel.

"You *are* my boss, but you're an animal doctor, not a people doctor," she argued . . . *and a pompous ass.*

"Makes no difference. You're going to the ER to be checked. As you pointed out, I am a DVM, not an MD, so I can't give you a clean bill-of-health."

"Okay," she grumbled, "my head hurts too much to argue."

With that, the paramedics loaded her onto the gurney, placing her personal belongings at her feet. As they rolled her toward the door, she heard the detective ask, "Is there any chance Ms. Morelli opened the pharmacy door to her assailant and then became his victim to hide her involvement?"

"Not a chance in hell," Jordan replied.

"Veterinary assistants don't have keys for the pharmacy."

"Who does?"

"My office manager and I."

"Well, that narrows the suspect list," Turner said. "Anybody upstairs with you in your apartment when this happened?"

"Nope."

"In the morning we'll see if the office manager has an alibi. Since we know you don't have one—as they say in the movies—don't leave town."

Had she been able, Kat would have smiled at the detective's quip, but even the thought of smiling hurt too much.

TWO

Detective Turner instructed the deputy to seal the pharmacy area with crime scene tape. "I'll be back in the morning to talk with your staff," he told Jordan. "Meanwhile, make a list of your enemies, people who might want to cause you or your business harm. If Ms. Morelli hadn't been attacked this would be a low priority crime, since so little was taken. Assault ramps this up from a misdemeanor B&E to a felony."

Jordan followed Turner and the deputy to the door and locked up.

After ushering them out, he headed straight to his car. He should have grabbed a jacket, he thought. In the high country, the chill of late summer nights in September warned that autumn was on the way. He ignored his discomfort and headed to the medical facility to make certain Kat was receiving skilled care. She'd been a spunky adversary when she'd challenged him. He hoped this episode wouldn't damage her spirit and send her rushing back to wherever she'd come from. As petite as she was, she might have been seriously injured.

The waiting room was empty when he arrived. From the receptionist he learned Kat was in an exam room, and he knew, since he wasn't family, he wouldn't be allowed to join her unless she asked for him.

"Who is treating her?" he demanded impatiently, "Scott Petersen or Mike Larsen?"

Both men had grown up with Jordan in the small town of Spruce Creek. All three had gone to the town's single high school. Scott had been in Jordan's older sister's class and had dated her briefly in their junior year. Mike had been a year behind Jordan, but they'd played varsity baseball together. After finishing their residencies, all three men had returned home to practice medicine for people or animals. They weren't bosom buddies—Jordan didn't *have* close friends—but they were well acquainted. Jordan hoped Petersen was on call. He believed him to be more experienced, given his five years seniority.

The receptionist gave Jordan a frosty stare. "Dr. Petersen is on rotation tonight."

"I want to talk to him as soon as he is available."

"And you are . . . ?" she asked pointedly.

"Tell him Jordan Walker wants to talk to him. I'm Ms. Morelli's employer, and she was injured on my premises."

Without pausing for a response, Jordan turned his back on the woman and strode across the waiting room. The walls had been painted an institutional green. Various medical posters were tacked about randomly—warnings concerning AIDS and HIV, posters declaring the community medical center to be a safe-haven for unwanted babies, and other notices questioning if someone was being hurt by a family member or friend. The waiting room furniture looked as uncomfortable as he knew his own visitor chairs to be.

He stood at the windows looking out to the parking lot wondering why he was even here. He knew the small facility was equipped to handle most minor medical emergencies. Major injuries and cardiac cases would be stabilized and medevaced down the mountain to the big-city hospital, but Kat's injury didn't appear life threatening. He would talk to Petersen, and then he'd go home and get some sleep.

As Jordan started to pace, Dr. Scott Petersen emerged from the treatment area. "Hello, Walker, what brings you here?"

"My SUV."

"Still a smart ass, I see."

"Seriously, your patient, Kat Morelli, is my employee. She was attacked at my clinic this evening. I want to make certain she's going to be okay."

"Is this concern for her as a person? Or are you afraid she's going to sue you?"

Jordan heard the dislike in Petersen's voice, but he didn't care about his opinion as long as he treated Kat well. "I'm concerned about Kat as a person. I'm not quite the bastard you think I am."

"In that case, since you know I can't disclose personal medical information to you, why don't you come back into the treatment area and speak with Ms. Morelli—if she's willing, that is."

Jordan followed Petersen through the door into the treatment area. The buzz of equipment and the ping of monitors emphasized this was not a restful place. Petersen stopped in front of a canvas curtain which covered the entry into a treatment space. "Ms. Morelli, your boss is here to check up on you. Do you wish to see him?"

"Dr. Walker's here? Oh yes, please."

At that, Petersen pulled the curtain open. "She's been sedated, so don't stay too long and don't get her agitated." He moved away from the cubicle, giving them a semblance of privacy.

Jordan was appalled by the purple bruise he saw developing around Kat's eye and along her jaw. There was a small wound above her hairline which seeped blood. He controlled his expression, not wanting her to know just how ugly her wounds appeared. She might think him unfeeling, but he didn't intend to reinforce her opinion by blurting out unpleasant truths.

Jordan took another step into the small treatment cubicle. Taking her hand, he again felt the spark between them. "How do you feel?"

"My head still hurts, and Dr. Petersen says I have a concussion. He wants to keep me overnight for observation," she replied sleepily.

"Well, then, you'll stay." Jordan spoke softly. "If you give Petersen permission, he can tell me how you're doing when I phone to check on you in the morning. When he releases you, we'll make certain you get home. You won't come back to work until he says you may."

"Dr. Walker, I haven't been working long enough for my health insurance to take effect. I can't afford to stay in a hospital, and I can't afford to miss work."

"Don't worry," he assured her. "The clinic will pay for your medical expenses, and you'll receive your full salary while you're at home recuperating."

Jordan turned to see Petersen standing at the nurse's station making entries into a computer—probably treatment notes. "Scott, please see that all Ms. Morelli's medical bills are sent to my clinic. We'll pay all expenses associated with this incident. Oh, and let me know when she's to be released."

Petersen turned to Kat. "Is this acceptable to you, Ms. Morelli?"

"Yes, Dr. Petersen," she said, swallowing a yawn. "Please give Dr. Walker any information he requests."

"Can he take your wallet and keys for safe keeping? He can leave your personal items, but we prefer not have patient valuables on site," Petersen continued.

Kat barely nodded her permission. "Dr. Walker, I apologize for all the trouble I've caused."

Jordan looked at her pixie face. She was so pale, her freckles looked like grains of sand scattered across her nose. She had a peculiar appeal which tugged at heart strings he didn't know he possessed. "You haven't caused any problems, Kat. The burglar is entirely responsible."

After accepting her keys and wallet, Jordan again took Kat's hand and squeezed gently. "I'll leave now and let you get some rest. Do you want me to contact your family?"

"Oh, no, please don't," Kat said in a panicked voice. She looked seriously distressed at the idea he might alert her family to her injuries.

Remembering Petersen's instructions and not wanting to cause her any more strife, he acquiesced. "As you wish. I'll see you tomorrow, either to take you home or to check on you."

"Good night, Dr. Walker. Thank you for coming." A smile touched her lips as her glacier-colored blue eyes drifted shut.

Jordan knew now why he had come to the hospital. He'd come for her smile.

THREE

When Kat awoke she had three pressing needs: a bathroom, a big drink of water, and a pain pill. She pressed the call button and, when the scratchy voice came over the intercom, she pleaded for help. A nurse came promptly and assisted her across the cold tile floor to the lavatory. When she got back into bed, she found a Vicodin and a pitcher of cold, fresh water waiting for her. She downed the pill with two large glasses of liquid. The water tasted fantastic, and she hoped the pain pill would kick in soon.

"Here's the menu from Jenny's," the nurse said. "Our food service is carry-in from the café across the street. What would you like for lunch?"

"I don't think I want food right now." Kat said. "My stomach doesn't feel so good."

"Can I tempt you with some cool sherbet or Jell-O? You should have something in your stomach with the meds you are taking."

"Oh, sherbet sounds good. What are my choices?"

"Orange or orange—which do you prefer?"

When the nurse came back with Kat's sherbet, she relayed the message that Dr. Walker had called and planned on coming by.

Kat was warmly pleased by the news until she gave thought to what she must look like. "Can someone come help me clean up? If I look as shabby as I feel, I must be a scary sight."

"I'll have an aide come in as soon as you've finished your sherbet. Then you'll probably want to rest again. Vicodin makes you drowsy, so you may drift off."

"Please wake me if I'm asleep when Dr. Walker arrives. I don't want to miss his visit. I want to know what's happening at the clinic—learn if they've found any leads to my attacker."

The aide arrived, discarded the empty sherbet container, and helped Kat into a sitting position. "What's your name?" Kat asked the woman.

"I'm Nancy," the aide replied. "What can I do to help you, dearie?"

"My boss will be coming by in a little while.

I'd like to freshen up before he gets here."

"Well, missy, if you are up to it, you can have a sponge bath, a fresh hospital gown, and a touch of make-up to brighten your appearance."

"Oh, please, yes," Kat responded, thinking it would feel good to be clean and fresh.

When her bed-bath was finished and she'd changed into a clean gown, Kat asked Nancy for a mirror so she could comb her hair and put on some lip gloss.

Nancy removed the basin from the tray table, wiped the surface dry, and then turned the tray top ninety degrees so a mirrored surface was facing Kat.

She groaned in disbelief when she saw her reflection. Her hair looked as if a family of sparrows had taken up residence. Gone were her neat russet braids, and instead her hair stuck out every which way. On her skull, high above her right eye, there was an angry red patch. Her hair had been shaved, and she had a nasty gash stitched with black silk. Her face looked as if she had been hit with a baseball bat. She had the beginnings of a black eye which would only get worse. Maybe she *should* be asleep when Jordan arrived.

Not seriously caring how she looked, she

tried, without much success, to gently run the comb through her hair.

"Here, honey, let me help you," Nancy insisted. She took the comb out of Kat's hand and picked up a brush instead. She took particular care when she neared the wound. When she finished, she drew Kat's hair back into a loose, thick braid.

Nancy handed Kat lip gloss and a small tube of hand cream. "Here you go. Hospital rooms are always too warm—dry everything out."

Kat thanked her for her kindness and watched in appreciation as Nancy quickly straightened the room, smoothed the sheets, and opened the curtain.

After Nancy departed, Kat adjusted her bed to a semi-reclining position and turned on the television. Daytime TV sucked, but it was better than staring at pale green walls and Venetian blinds. Perhaps the drone from daytime game shows would lull her back to sleep.

She was just drifting off when Dr. Petersen walked in.

He parted her hair and inspected the stitches. "Not bad needlework, if I do say so myself."

Next he pulled up her eyelids and looked into her eyes with a bright light. "So how do you feel this afternoon?"

"No reflection on your medical skills, doctor, but I feel as if I've been dragged a mile behind a fast-moving horse. I just want to go home, take a shower, lie on a chaise, and eat bonbons."

Petersen laughed. "Not going to happen today, Ms. Morelli. Your eyes are still slightly dilated, and I want to watch your wound to make certain it doesn't become infected. No showers until those stitches are gone. And you don't strike me as the type to eat bonbons. One more night here, and I'll probably release you tomorrow."

"Are you serious? I can't go home today even if I promise not to take a shower, lie on a chaise, or eat bonbons?"

"I'm afraid not. You're here until at least Wednesday."

As Jordan approached Kat's room, he overheard Scott Petersen's last comment telling her she would be staying at least one more day. He stepped to the side of the hallway and waited for Scott Petersen to leave his patient.

"Scott," he hissed as the doctor left the room, "over here. Why are you keeping Kat another day?" he asked when Petersen approached.

"Most concussed patients are released after just one overnight."

"Ms. Morelli is not most patients," the doctor replied. "Her bills are not being paid by an insurance company or PPO that fights every second of patient hospitalization. Her eyes are still slightly dilated, which troubles me a little. And she tells me that when she returns home, she'll be alone without anyone to take care of her. Those are three compelling reasons for me to keep her here."

"Okay, I was concerned something more serious was the cause."

"Well, I'll be honest—I don't like that her eyes are still slightly dilated. So I'm going to keep a close watch on her. I'll check her again this evening. Go talk to her and cheer her up."

"Thanks, Scott," Jordan said. "She just started working for me and she doesn't deserve what happened to her."

"Be careful, Walker. People might suspect you have a heart buried somewhere beneath all your disdain. You don't want to ruin your reputation."

"She's my employee, nothing more." Jordan hoped he was being truthful.

At least she'd been moved from the small treatment cubicle in the ER into a patient room with a real bed. There were only three patient beds in the small clinic. Those, combined with the ER area which was also used for minor outpatient surgeries, encompassed the *hospital* portion of the building. The doctors' offices and exam rooms were in another wing.

As he turned to enter Kat's room, Jordan schooled his features so as not to register dismay at her appearance. Recalling how she had looked the night before, he knew her bruises would be worse today.

"Well, Ms. Morelli, are you feeling at all better today?"

Kat turned her face to him. "Before I answer your question, I'm going to make a request. Please call me Kat, okay? You call Torrey by her first name—you should do the same for me. Please."

"I've known Torrey a lot longer than I've known you," Jordan said, stiffening into his hands-off demeanor. "I don't wish to appear disrespectful or act inappropriately."

"Addressing me by my first name is neither disrespectful nor inappropriate."

He nodded. "Okay—Kat are you feeling better today?"

"Not especially. I ache all over, my head feels

ready to explode, and I'm tired and sleepy all the time."

Jordan nodded solemnly, unable to relax in her presence. "I'm certain that being tired and sleepy is the result of your medications. We keep recovering animals sedated to hasten their healing, as you well know. People aren't any different."

"I'm frustrated. Dr. Petersen isn't going to let me go home today. Another day in the hospital is going to cost you more money."

"The clinic has both comprehensive loss and liability insurance, Kat. My insurer will be paying the bills, not me. And, unlike cases controlled by medical insurance dictates, Dr. Petersen will determine how long you should stay in the hospital, not a tight-fisted PPO. So, set your mind at ease and just concentrate on getting well."

"Yes, sir," she replied, bowing to his higher authority with a gamin grin on her face.

She was cute, he thought, in spite of the ugly bruise. But she did have a sharp tongue. He'd need to watch himself.

"Now that we know the extent of your injuries and that you're going to recover, would you like me to get in touch with your family? I'm sure they'd want to be here for you."

"No. Don't contact them," Kat asserted. "My parents would be convinced I was responsible for what happened. I don't want to listen to them criticize me for causing problems again."

"Surely you can't be serious," Jordan said, looking at her in astonishment. "You weren't at fault. You were doing your job and found yourself in the wrong place at the wrong time. You probably saved the clinic from a greater loss by interrupting the burglary."

"You don't know my parents," Kat said. "If anything goes wrong, I'm at fault. They consider me a perpetual screw-up. I'm inadequate in every way. I do nothing right, unlike my brother who can do no wrong."

Jordan didn't know how to respond. He didn't have heart-to-heart talks with his employees. They didn't pour out their relationship problems in his hearing. He felt extremely uncomfortable at Kat's confession of parental disapproval.

"As you wish, I won't inform your family since your injuries aren't life threatening. You're an adult, presumably, and entitled to your privacy. I'll have Torrey make a note on your employment documents not to get in touch with your next of kin without your permission."

"Thank you, Dr. Walker. Your cooperation relieves my mind, and I'm certain will help speed my recovery. I don't want my parents' interference."

As Jordan prepared to depart, another thought occurred to him. "If you're unable to call on family to help you when you're released from the hospital, Dr. Petersen may refuse to discharge you. Do you have friends who can help out?"

"I've only been in Spruce Creek a few weeks," Kat said. "I don't know anyone except a couple of neighbors and the people I've met at the clinic. So no, I don't have friends who can help out. I'll be fine taking care of myself; nobody needs to worry about me."

"Dr. Petersen may disagree. But I'll ask Torrey to work on the problem. She'll find a solution."

FOUR

Jordan was flabbergasted, "Torrey, you're out of your mind. Kat can't move into my apartment."

"Of course she can, Jordan," Torrey calmly insisted. "Having her in your apartment solves all the problems presented by her release from the hospital. She'll be close at hand. You and I can check on her as often as necessary. If she needs help, we're only seconds away."

Torrey continued filing, completely ignoring Jordan's agitation. "If Kat's assailant believes she can identify him and thinks to harm her, your presence will discourage him. There are two bedrooms in the apartment, so you won't need to sleep on the couch. And everybody in this town knows what a Popsicle you are, so it's not as if anyone is going to accuse you of inappropriate behavior. Kat's reputation will be perfectly safe."

"Popsicle—what do you mean everyone knows what a Popsicle I am?"

"Jordan, you've been back in Spruce Creek ever since you received your license. In all that time, you haven't dated one single female in this town or anywhere else, for that matter. You are a cold stick. For all anyone knows, you might be gay."

"I'm not gay, and you know it," Jordan sputtered. "I just don't trust women. You know what my mother did. I'm not going to open myself up to that kind of heartbreak again. I have you and my sister. You two are the only women I trust. I don't need a relationship with any other woman."

"That statement supports my comment that Kat's reputation is safe if she stays with you." Torrey turned to Jordan and stretched out her hands. "You don't have a relationship with anyone. You avoided your father before he died. You don't reach out to your brother and sister. You don't have any male buddies that you hang with. You growl at your employees. You are disagreeable to the pet owners. If the next nearest vet wasn't twenty miles away, you probably wouldn't even have a clinic practice. Look how poorly you treated Mr. Gardner the other day."

The sad disapproval written on Torrey's face caused him to pull back. "I did not treat Gardner poorly. I just defended how I choose to run my practice," he said. "I need to make an adequate income to keep the clinic viable, to pay your salary and the rest of the staff. If I'm forced to close my doors, the people of this town will be driving those twenty miles to get treatment for their pets."

"I know your financial status, Jordan. The Spruce Creek Veterinary Clinic is soundly in the black. That's not the problem. The problem is your attitude."

He heard what she was saying, but he didn't want to believe it. "I don't need to stand for this kind of criticism, not even from you." He turned and stormed off.

While Jordan was angry with Torrey for pointing out his shortcomings, he knew she was right. He didn't care about much. He treated the local animals because that was his job, but he didn't have any empathy for their owners. He had no connection to his employees; he easily could replace any of them—except Torrey. He knew he couldn't replace Torrey.

He had come home to Spruce Creek when he received his license because he loved the environment. He enjoyed living in the mountains and experiencing four distinct seasons. But he didn't have any connection to the community. Taking over his father's clinic was simply easier than starting from scratch somewhere he wasn't known. His father had suffered a stroke during Jordan's final year in school, and then, after Jordon took over the practice, he passed on. Jordan felt guilty that he didn't feel any sense of loss.

His father, Old Doc Walker, had always cared about the people as much as the animals. What did it get him? The old doc didn't charge enough to support a family, and what he did charge, he didn't always collect. As a result, his wife and children did without. When his father wouldn't or couldn't change, Jordan's mother packed up and left. Three motherless children were abandoned and didn't understand why. The farmhouse across the road from the clinic ceased to be a home and turned into a shell occupied by a sad, lonely man and three bewildered kids. Jordan was six years old when his mother went away. His sister, Jessica, was ten. His younger brother, Jeremy, was eighteen months.

Jessie did her best to be a little mother, but it was too much to ask of a ten-year old with a father who didn't understand and couldn't accept his wife's departure. Jessie and Jordan were in school most of the day, but the toddler Jeremy was brought to the clinic and cared for in a haphazard way by the clinic staff. He was just one more puppy to be petted and cuddled by anyone with a free minute.

When Torrey came to work for Doc Walker, she assumed responsibility for managing the children, as well as the clinic. The apartment above the clinic was made habitable and she lived there until the kids no longer needed a surrogate mother. While the children were young, when they came in from school, she would meet them upstairs with a warm hug and a snack. She expected the Walker kids to do their homework. Torrey went to parent-teacher conferences. She imposed discipline on three unruly hooligans. She did her best to act *in loco parentis.*

When their homework was complete, the children were expected to come downstairs to the clinic and pitch in. Jessie didn't particularly like working with wounded or sick animals, so she helped out on the clerical side. Jordan learned veterinary medicine on the job following behind his dad. Jeremy, when he was old enough, did menial labor cleaning cages, walking dogs, feeding and watering recovering animals. When the day was done, four disconnected souls traipsed across the road to a building that housed their beds, but not the spirit of a family.

Thanks to Torrey they didn't have a miserable childhood, but it was unconventional and not especially happy. Doc Walker was out of touch with his kids. He did for them whatever he was told to do by his office manager, stumbling along, a broken and disillusioned man.

In her search for love, his sister Jessica made what she mistakenly believed was a poor marriage. Jordan didn't agree. He thought Matt Whitaker was an admirable man, one who would do anything for Jessie.

In his search for identity, his brother Jeremy wandered without direction. Jordan wasn't sure where his brother spent his time or what he did to keep his pockets lined. But he never seemed in need of money, so Jordan didn't concern himself.

Jordan didn't accept that he personally needed to search for anything. But while he couldn't point to any specific lack, he knew he wasn't happy with things as they were. So perhaps Torrey was right, and he should be searching for a new attitude.

What did any of this have to do with Kat coming to stay at his apartment when she was discharged in the afternoon? Was reality such that no one, not even Torrey, believed he could be attracted to a lovely woman living under the same roof with him? Perhaps they were right, or maybe—just maybe—they were wrong.

FIVE

After listening to Scott Petersen instruct Jordan that he was to bring her back on Friday for a follow up visit, and telling him that she could not drive nor return to work until the next Monday, Kat felt as if she were twelve years old. The two men talked about her as if she were incapable of taking care of herself. Still, she settled into the comfortable passenger seat of the BMW because it was transportation.

The new-car smell mingled with the scent of Jordan's aftershave, fresh and crisp. A muted sound of strength escaped quietly from the sturdy 300 horsepower engine. The sunny afternoon returned her to her normal sunny disposition.

She was glad Jordan hadn't brought the big SUV used for transporting injured or stray animals. Climbing into the oversized truck would have presented difficulties. She wasn't as strong as she wished, and instead of wearing long pants, she was dressed in the skirt and blouse that Torrey had sent to the hospital with Jordan. The clothes she'd been wearing when she was admitted, splotched with her dried blood, had been taken into evidence by the deputies.

As Jordan steered the car out of the hospital parking lot, Kat focused on his strong hands gripping the steering wheel. She turned toward him with a smile. "Thank you for coming to fetch me, Dr. Walker," she said. "But you didn't need to do it yourself—you could have sent someone else, or I could have called for a taxi."

"There *are* no taxis in Spruce Creek. People either drive themselves, or are driven by friends and relatives. "

"Oh. Then please, take me to the clinic so I can get my car and drive myself home."

"I *am* taking you to the clinic, but you will *not* be driving yourself home or anywhere else. You heard Dr. Petersen. Torrey insists we keep you where she can take care of you. You'll be staying in my apartment upstairs over the clinic."

"But where will you go?"

"I'm not going anywhere. The apartment has

two bedrooms, and Torrey assures me your reputation will not suffer because no one in this town believes that I could do anything inappropriate. So you'll be perfectly safe."

Kat was prepared to argue, but Jordan told her to take it up with his office manager. He didn't think she would be any more successful than he had been.

When they arrived at the clinic, he showed her up the stairs, pointed out her bedroom, and told her to make herself at home.

She was still sputtering when he descended to let Torrey know that a displeased Kat was waiting.

Kat heard Torrey hastening up the stairs to the apartment. The office manager had no sooner walked through the door when Kat started to berate her. "Torrey, I don't even like Dr. Walker. I may need to tolerate him because he's the boss, but I sure as hell don't want to live with him."

As Jordan had predicted, Kat was no more persuasive than he had been at changing Torrey's mind. "Relax child, he'll grow on you."

"What? Grow on me like a fungus?"

Torrey laughed as she showed Kat the location of her things. The woman had retrieved clothing, cosmetics, and personal items from

Kat's little apartment and settled them into the room that was to be hers.

Torrey led her into the kitchen and opened the refrigerator door. "Help yourself to whatever you like," she said. "Everything is fresh and healthy. All the food you see is organic and as process-free as humanly possible—no hormones, preservatives, or artificial coloring—you get the idea."

"Does Dr. Walker cook all this food for himself?"

"Yes, Jordan does cook for himself. Sometimes his sister comes in and cooks a meal for him. She's out of town now, has been for a long time, so Jordan's on his own. He gets by," Torrey said. "You are not to worry about him. You can nap, or read, or watch TV. You are to take it easy. The phone up here is in Jordan's bedroom. It's an extension of the clinic telephone system, so if you need anything dial zero-one-one and you'll get me or my voice mail." Torrey departed down the stairs, leaving Kat to her own devices.

Kat wandered about the apartment, which was more spacious than she had expected. It had the same square footage as the clinic below. The layout wasn't particularly inspired, but it was functional: two bedrooms, one bath; living room, kitchen, and dining room; home office and a small laundry room.

Out of curiosity, since her new roommate was still down in the clinic, she opened the door to Jordan's bedroom and stuck her head in, *just to find the phone.* The space was neat and tidy, almost sterile. There were no pictures on the beige walls. The tops of the walnut dresser and bureau were both clear of knick-knacks and free of dust. Dark brown drapes hung to the sides of off-white sheers that covered the window; a patterned throw rug of the same dull colors rested on the hardwood floor at the side of the bed. Only a few books with bright covers resting on the night stand provided any relief from the depressing surroundings, but a hint of his fresh scent lingered. Kat had seen motel rooms with more personality.

She closed the door to Jordan's bedroom and ventured into the bathroom. She was met with the same sterile neatness. She decided right then that only her toothbrush and toothpaste would take up residence in his bathroom. Cosmetics, deodorant, hair brush and all similar items that would have been found in her bathroom at home would stay in the bedroom assigned to her.

Kat returned to the living room and perused the books found in Jordan's one and only bookcase. Obviously, he kept his veterinary books in his office. She found a selection of popular thriller and mystery writers—Harlan Coben, Michael Connelly, Vince Flynn, Stuart Woods, and others—but no female authors, nor books with female protagonists. She picked up a copy of *The Shape Shifter* by Tony Hillerman.

Stretched out on the couch, a bowl of dried mixed fruit at her elbow on the nearby coffee table, she began to read. She acknowledged to herself that she was tired and weaker than she was willing to admit. It felt fantastic to stretch out on Jordan's overstuffed sofa with a throw pillow under her head. A window was open somewhere in the apartment, and she could hear the chirps and trills of nearby birds. Occasionally she heard a dog bark or the sound of a car outside. She was quite content in her peaceful surroundings.

Her eyes grew heavy, and she closed them for just a minute. She laid the book on her chest to rest her arms. When she did, she drifted off musing about Jordan Walker. Physically, he had a body that would cause grown women to drool— tall, six feet at least, with dark brown hair cut short. His broad shoulders and strong arms looked equally capable of lifting a large animal or holding a woman close. When he thought he was unobserved, his big brown eyes gentled as he looked at his furry patients. They looked more like steel daggers when they rested on people.

JORDAN ENTERED THE APARTMENT, passed through the kitchen, and stopped short—he was disturbed by the image of Kat sleeping on his living room couch. Her skirt had ridden up above her knees, and the top button of her blouse was undone. He might not want a relationship, but he was male and she was attractive.

He knew having Kat here was a dreadful idea. But he didn't know how to convince Torrey. And now, with Kat settled in, he couldn't exactly evict her without raising all kinds of other questions and problems. So he would focus on the fact that she was an employee and off-limits.

He must have stood staring too long because Kat opened her eyes and looked directly into his. Recovering quickly, he said, "I'm sorry, I didn't mean to wake you."

She smiled and sat up. "I didn't expect to fall asleep. I guess I am not as recovered as I thought." Then she stood and stretched, and

Jordan found he needed to turn away.

The mantra kept repeating in his mind, *not good, not good at all . . .*

He walked back into the kitchen and began busying himself with preparations for dinner. He put wild rice on the stove to cook and pulled chicken breasts from the refrigerator. He began to season them before putting them in the oven to bake. "Dinner should be ready in an hour," he called to her.

In a few minutes, Kat followed him into the kitchen. "Dr. Walker, what can I do to help? I feel badly that you've worked all day, and now you're cooking dinner for me."

"Kat, sit down," he snapped at her.

She started to stammer an apology for whatever she had done to upset him, but he didn't give her a chance.

"Kat," he said, softening his tone, "we're going to be living together for whatever amount of time is necessary for you to recover and for the man who attacked you to be caught. Torrey pointed out that if he thinks you can identify him, you may be in danger. So you'll stay here where you can be protected. With that in mind, will you stop calling me Dr. Walker and start calling me Jordan? Can you do that?"

"Yes, sir," she replied, her eyes big and round.

Damn, he had intimidated her. That wasn't his intention.

"You are not to feel badly that I'm cooking. I cook every night, and there is no effort involved in putting a second chicken breast in the oven. Okay?"

"Okay."

"If you want to help, you can make a salad or set the table, whichever you prefer."

"May I do both . . . Jordan?" She hesitated slightly at the use of his first name.

"Yes, you may do both," he said, smiling in spite of his desire not to. "Start with setting the table. We'll eat here in the kitchen. I rarely use the dining room."

With an occasional direction from Jordan, Kat set the kitchen table and tossed a salad. Jordan served the hot foods directly from the stove. They sat across the table from each other without a word being spoken.

He decided that since this was his home and his kitchen, he should try to act like a host and start a conversation. If he didn't do something, the silent meal would be uncomfortable, and he didn't think added stress would help with their digestions.

"So, Kat," he began, "tell me about yourself."

"What do you want to know?"

"Where are you from? Why veterinary medicine? How did you end up in Spruce Creek?"

"I grew up on the plains in Fort Morgan," she answered. "I like animals and I seem to have an affinity with them. I wanted to live in the mountains, and there was an opportunity here in Spruce Creek. I applied, and Torrey hired me."

Jordan could see that maintaining a conversation was going be difficult. Kat wasn't volunteering any information. She answered precisely what was asked and nothing more.

"What was it like growing up on the plains?

"Probably much the same as growing up anywhere," she replied. "I went to school—tried to avoid my parents' control—for fun I hung out with friends or went to movies. There was no shopping center nearer than Greeley, so hanging out at the mall was not an option."

"It sounds boring," Jordan commented.

"It is," Kat continued. "You can't spend a lot of time outdoors even if there were stuff to do. The conditions are always windy and dusty. You can ride horses, go fishing or bird watching, and play golf. There are lots of golf courses around Fort Morgan. My dad plays at least twice a week.

I spent my time reading. In books I found a freedom of sorts, and the library had air conditioning."

"What about your family? Besides playing golf what does your dad do? And your mother, does she work? You mentioned having a brother." Jordan was trying to keep the conversation going, but getting Kat to speak freely was like pouring molasses out of a boot in January.

"Both my parents are teachers. Dad teaches high school science. Mom teaches middle school English. My brother is Mr. Perfect."

Jordan could tell that Kat was uncomfortable with his questions. She clearly resented her brother, so he would drop that line of conversation. "How is dinner?" he asked.

"Dinner is fantastic," Kat responded enthusiastically, obviously relieved at having a change in topic. "I can taste the difference from processed foods. Torrey says that you only eat organic."

Jordan could embrace talking about organic and non-processed food all evening. The conversation would keep going without more intrusive questions. He began telling Kat about which ranches raised grass-fed beef and cage-free chickens and where he could buy organic fruits and vegetables. He heaped praise on Jack Rabbit Hill Wines, naturally fermented, organic, and produced in western Colorado. He would be certain to give her the opportunity to sample the local vintage.

They worked together clearing the table and then they settled in the living room. Each of them picked a book to read. No further conversation was likely.

Jordan felt strange and a little lonely when Kat said good night and departed for the guest room. *Not good,* he reflected. *Not good at all.*

SIX

K at awoke suddenly, feeling anxious in the darkened room. Her heart pounded as she glanced at the clock on the nightstand; the illuminated numbers showed the time to be barely past midnight. She was unsure of what had roused her, but something had. Maybe the building was settling, or a window was rattling, or maybe the burglar had returned for her. She held her breath and listened warily.

In the weeks she'd been staying with Jordan she'd been sleeping soundly—feeling safe, secure, and untroubled. She strained to hear a repeat of the noise. Deciding the disturbance was her imagination, she sank back against her pillow, trying to settle her nerves and return to sleep. Suddenly the bedroom door was thrown open.

Kat screamed when the overhead light blinked on.

A strange man stood in the doorway.

"Who are you?" Kat demanded boldly, her voice showing none of the fear she was experiencing. She reached for the cell phone on the nightstand. She was ready to dial nine-one-one if she could control her shaking fingers. The sheriff couldn't get here in time to prevent the guy from harming her if that is what he had in mind, but maybe they would be in time to catch him before he could get away.

"I should be asking you that question since you're sleeping in my bed. Should I call you Goldilocks?" he asked as he strode into the room.

Then Jordan was in the doorway wearing nothing but black boxer briefs. "Kat, what's wrong?"

Overwhelmed, Kat dropped the phone, but found she was unable to answer either of the two men.

"Well, big brother," the stranger said, "who's this you have tucked away in my bed?"

"Jeremy. I might have known that you'd show up at the worst possible time. And it's only your bed when you're staying with me, which you are not." Jordan sounded exasperated. "Why didn't you call and let me know you were coming into town?"

"Because I didn't know I would be interrupting anything," Jeremy said.

Jordan sighed. "Kat, this is my little brother, Jeremy. He is the black sheep of the family."

Jeremy looked in Kat's direction with a wicked grin on his face.

"Jeremy, this is Kathleen Morelli. She's one of my veterinary techs, and she's staying here under my protection." Jordan turned to his brother. "If you want to bunk here tonight, you can sleep on the couch."

"What, I can't sleep in my own bed with the pretty lady?"

Jordan grabbed Jeremy by the shirt collar and dragged him from the room. "Good night, Kat. I'm sorry that Jeremy frightened you. We'll see you in the morning." Jordan turned off the light and closed the door.

Kat lay in bed with her heart racing like a skateboard rolling down hill. It would be a long while before her pulse returned to normal. She could hear the murmur of voices from beyond the door and the sound of a soft chuckle. Must be Jeremy, she thought. She'd never heard Jordan express any sound of humor.

In her mind, she immediately started planning to return to her own place. There was no way that she would remain in Jordan's apartment if his brother was going to be here. She could pack her belongings in the morning before going down the stairs to work in the clinic. Then at day's end she would throw her stuff in her car and drive across town to where she belonged.

Having to leave was unfortunate, because once she'd become adjusted, she found she liked sharing Jordan's apartment in spite of her personal dislike for the man—which, if she were honest, had lessened significantly. His space was more comfortable than her rental, the commute to work was nonexistent, and Jordan was quiet and undemanding. She only saw him at breakfast and dinner. The rest of the time they went about their own pursuits. She ran into him in the course of the work day, but then he was the doctor and she was the assistant. He had loosened up toward her, but they still didn't spend much time in small talk. Every once in awhile she would catch him staring at her, but then quickly he would look away.

She usually fixed breakfast, and he cooked dinner; they each looked after themselves at lunch. Jordan set the table before all their shared meals and Kat cleaned up after. Jordan had a housekeeper who came in once a week to change the linens, vacuum the floors, and clean the bathroom. Never a fan of housework, Kat admitted to herself she would miss being free of chores.

As she closed her eyes, an image of Jordan wearing only sexy underwear was burned into her retinas. In spite of the close quarters, they had both avoided appearing partially dressed in front of the other. She didn't blame Jordan for his scanty attire—he was simply reacting to her scream—but she was surprised to find that he was so hot. She had never dreamed that under his conservative vet's attire lurked a hunk. The sight of his naked torso, tight and lean with cords of muscles in his arms and shoulders, aroused her. His dark brown hair had been mussed, and his big brown eyes had smoldered with challenge as he readied to attack whatever had frightened her.

Jeremy might be the one who suggested sharing her bed, but Jordan was the one she would invite.

Where had that thought come from? She didn't even like Jordan Walker. She pinched herself to divert her thoughts from sexy male images. She was behaving like a silly teenage girl, panting after the latest teen idol. Jordan was her boss, not a potential lover. He respected her as a veterinary tech, but he didn't like her as a woman. She didn't believe he liked or trusted any woman. Kat didn't know the story behind his attitude, but his dislike of the female species was fairly obvious.

She needed to stay focused on her job, help the sheriff's department find the burglar who had attacked her, and get on with her life.

SEVEN

In the morning, Kat rose earlier than usual. She hurried her shower with the intention of packing her belongings before she started preparing breakfast. As she came out of the bathroom wrapped in an oversized terrycloth robe, she collided with Jeremy who was headed in. The towel she had wrapped around her wet hair fell to the floor. She bent to retrieve it. When she straightened up, she saw Jeremy's eyes fastened on her cleavage.

"Too bad I'm in a hurry," he said in a husky early morning voice. "I'd sure like to stay and enjoy the view."

Kat could feel her face flush as she pushed past him into her bedroom. She shut the door firmly. There was no lock on her door, so she had to trust that Jeremy was only being a tease and that he wouldn't intrude on her privacy. She dressed hurriedly, nonetheless, in scrub pants and a flowered smock. She toweled her hair dry and plaited it into a single braid. Gathering her clothes and personal items, she tossed them into the suitcase Torrey had used to bring her things from her apartment. There wasn't a lot to pack, so she made quick work of it. She set her suitcase outside the door.

Her good spirits renewed, Kat hummed as she went about her morning routine in the kitchen. She set the fair trade coffee to brewing, inhaling the scent. Nothing smelled better than coffee early in the morning. She slipped apple maple sausages into the skillet. Brown-shelled eggs from a nearby farmer who raised cage-free chickens were also on the menu.

Once, when Kat had gone with Jordan to get eggs, the farmer told her funny stories about the strange places his chickens chose to lay. He told of having to climb into a culvert to retrieve breakfast one morning. He insisted that every day was a treasure hunt.

Kat set about chopping vegetables for an omelet. She found pleasure in the bright colors and crisp freshness of Jordan's organic produce and in the aroma of fresh chopped onions and bell peppers. She sliced the home-baked bread she'd made the day before, and popped it into the toaster. Instead of waiting for Jordan to set the table, she did it herself and was ready to serve breakfast when the two brothers walked into the kitchen.

Jeremy and Jordan sat at the table, and Kat served up three plates directly from the stove.

"You still eat only organic food, big brother?" Jeremy asked.

"Absolutely," Jordan nodded vigorously. "When you finish eating this morning, try to convince me that you have had a better breakfast anywhere on the planet."

The two men bickered good-naturedly back and forth. Kat had never seen Jordan so relaxed. She felt like an intruder.

When everyone finished, she cleared the table, rinsed the dishes, and put them into the dishwasher. She was ready to head downstairs to work when Jordan returned to the kitchen with Jeremy right behind him.

"Why is your suitcase in the hallway?" Jordan asked her.

"I can't stay here with your brother moving in," she said, surprised he even had to ask. "I packed my stuff. I'll return to my place after work this afternoon."

"You are not going anywhere. My sister has an unoccupied house in Spruce Creek. And my father's house across the road is still standing empty. Jeremy can bunk in either one."

"But . . ."

"Do you want to tell Torrey you are leaving our protection?" Jordan asked, cutting off her protest.

"Well, no, not exactly." Kate had developed a healthy respect for Torrey Hansen, especially since Torrey ordered Jordan around just like she did everyone else.

"I don't mean to interrupt," Jeremy said. "Can someone explain to me why Kat needs protection?"

Jordan told Jeremy about the break-in some weeks earlier. He explained that Kat was a witness, though she didn't consciously remember anything because the intruder had knocked her out. But everyone involved—Torrey, Jordan, the sheriff, everyone except Kat herself—felt she needed to be protected until the burglary had been solved.

"So, what do the cops have so far?" Jeremy asked.

"Not much," Jordan replied in disgust. "So far they've hinted that I'm the most likely suspect."

"Then why are they letting Kat stay here?" he asked, raising his eyebrows.

"Because if anything happens to her, they'll know for sure I'm the guilty party."

"Dumb," Jeremy said. "I'll nose around and see what I can find out."

Jordan shook his head. "Jeremy, stay out of it. Let the law do their thing."

"Hey, I'm the black sheep, remember? I know people in this county the sheriff hasn't even heard of, and people will talk to me before they will any police investigator."

Kat listened to the back and forth between the two men. "Jeremy, you weren't even here when the burglary took place. I don't think you can be of much help. I agree with Jordan, just let the sheriff handle this."

Jeremy looked at his brother. "Is she always this outspoken?"

"You should have heard her when she first came to work here. She jumped all over my case about charging senior citizens too much money because I didn't offer a senior discount."

Kat felt the heat in her face and knew she was blushing. She was embarrassed all over again when she remembered her first confrontation with Jordan.

The brothers carried on their conversation as if she were not present. "She doesn't look big enough to give you much trouble," Jeremy said.

"She's not," Jordan agreed, "but that doesn't seem to stop her. If she had a lick of sense, she would have run the other way when she saw the light in the pharmacy. But she didn't—she just rushed right in to confront the burglar, and got knocked unconscious as a result. She's big trouble in a small package."

"Stop!" Kat demanded, stomping her foot. "It's rude to talk about me as if I'm not here."

Kat turned on her heel and slammed the door behind her as she started down the stairs to the clinic.

"SHE'S A FIERY LITTLE PACKAGE," Jeremy said after Kat's explosive exit from the apartment.

"Don't get any ideas, little brother. She's not for the likes of you."

"Are you staking a claim?" Jeremy asked, looking bemused.

"You know me better than that. I'm not interested in her as a woman. She's just too innocent, too sweet, to be thrown to the wolves. So don't start pursuing her."

"At the risk of misquoting Will Shakespeare, 'Methinks thou doth protest too much.' " Jeremy replied.

Jordan shook his head in frustration. "You don't understand. She's a valuable employee. She has a very calming way with the animals and with their owners. My practice is running smoother since she has started working here. If it weren't for the pharmacy burglary, I would say things couldn't be better." Jordan looked at his brother to see if he was getting his message. "I don't want to lose her."

"All this praise and you're telling me you have no interest in Kat as a woman. Jordan, you're lying to me and to yourself. I've never seen you so protective of any woman, not even Jessie. Wake up, big brother."

"Jeremy, I don't trust women, you know that. I never will."

"You trust Torrey."

"That's different."

"Why?"

"Because Torrey is trustworthy. She's proven herself."

"And Kat—is it possible that she also might

be trustworthy?"

"This conversation is getting out of hand. I'm going to work."

Jordan departed down the steps to the clinic every bit as disconcerted as Kat had been, but without the fireworks.

He jumped right into his work, clearing his mind of the conversation with his brother. The day proceeded much as he anticipated. He had two surgeries—one spay and one neuter—both cats. Jordan treated the normal number of pet illnesses and injuries, both real and imagined. He administered vaccines and did well-pet exams.

When he found himself working with Kat, he thought about the morning's conversation with Jeremy. He admitted to himself he was attracted to her. She was no pushover. She spoke her mind, but she wasn't selfish. She treated her co-workers with respect. She did her share of the distasteful tasks as well as the more pleasant ones. He knew she had taken some flack because she was living in his apartment, but she laughed it off and went on about her job.

But he wasn't about to let any woman into his life. Not now, not ever.

EIGHT

Detective Turner showed up at the clinic on Tuesday in the mid-afternoon to talk to Kat. Jordan surrendered his office to them so they could have privacy.

"Ms. Morelli, have you remembered anything more about the attack?" Turner asked, settling uncomfortably into one of the guest chairs.

"I'm afraid not," Kat said, shaking her head.

Then she remembered the scent. "Detective, I don't remember that night very clearly, but there was a smell—an odor I didn't recognize. Did I mention that at the time the deputies took the report?"

Turner thumbed through the incident report. "I don't see any mention of an unidentified odor. What kind of scent? When did you smell it?"

"I couldn't immediately identify it. It was kind of spicy. I think I noticed it as soon as I walked into the back of the clinic, before I approached the pharmacy. I don't remember anything more than that."

"Ms. Morelli, would you be willing to undergo hypnosis to help us on this case? Park County has a psychologist on call who has been very successful at uncovering submerged memories for some of our victims."

"Would he ask questions about anything other than the attack?"

"Our psychologist is a woman, and no, she won't ask about anything other than the attack," Turner said with a smile. "Don't worry—your secrets will be safe."

Kat felt herself blush once again. "Who would be present while I'm being questioned?"

"I'll be there, along with the psychologist and a technician who'll record the questions and answers. Is there someone else you'd like to be present?"

Jordan . . . the thought caught her off guard. Without being aware of it, she'd come to depend on him for moral support. But if he were there, she might reveal something about her growing feelings for him. That would be worse than embarrassing—such a revelation would be a disaster.

"I don't think Dr. Walker's presence would be appropriate, since he remains our only suspect," Turner said, as if he were reading her mind.

"Detective Turner, I don't for a second believe that Jordan Walker had anything to do with the attack. You can get that thought right out of your head," she said. "But for my own reasons, I agree that he shouldn't be present."

"If I can arrange with the psychologist for the hypnosis to take place tomorrow or the next day, will that be convenient?"

"Where will I need to go?"

"Her offices are in Denver. I realize that is some distance for you to travel, but you'll be more comfortable there than at the sheriff's office or the district station."

"Go ahead and set up an appointment. Let me know when and where, and I'll be there. The sooner we get this done, the sooner I can get my life back to normal."

Turner left and Kat sat quietly for a moment. Jordan came through the door into his office. "Is everything okay?" he asked.

Kat looked up. "Everything's fine, except that dunce still thinks you're responsible for the attack. He's making arrangements for a psychologist to hypnotize me to see if she can recover any memories I may have stuck in my subconscious. I'll need to go to Denver to her office."

"I'll drive you," Jordan insisted. "You aren't going anywhere unescorted."

"You won't be able to be there during the session."

"That's okay, I'll wait for you."

Kat thought of all the things Jordan had done for her. She still loathed his behavior at times, but she also knew she was becoming attracted to him. And when he did nice things for her, she began to believe that perhaps he was attracted to her, as well—probably wishful thinking.

NINE

D etective Turner was waiting for Kat when she and Jordan entered the psychologist's reception area on Thursday morning. Kat took note of the serene setting—ivory colored walls with tranquil prints, overstuffed furniture upholstered in a beige knobby fabric, no harsh or garish colors, no disturbing décor, all softly designed to calm a troubled spirit.

Jordan was obviously paying no attention to his surroundings. "How long will this take?" he asked, barely acknowledging Turner's greeting.

"Probably an hour," Turner replied.

"I'll plan on being back by then. But if I'm not, don't let her leave here alone."

"She's not a prisoner, Dr. Walker. I can't force her to stay if she wishes to leave."

"You're doing it again Jordan—talking about me as if I weren't standing right here," Kat snapped.

"Sorry," Jordan replied.

"I'll wait for you. But stop treating me as if I were one of your patients. I'm not a pampered pet without control over my own life."

Kat had surprised herself, barking at Jordan like that. *When had she grown fangs?* Her outspoken self-assurance first began when she started working at the clinic and had expanded the longer she stayed. This was not the first time she had growled at Jordan, but never before in public. *Had she developed this new attitude because she was away from the influence of her parents? Did she like this new Kathleen Morelli?* She thought maybe she did.

Her brief introspective was interrupted by a middle aged, motherly looking woman.

"Ms. Morelli, I'm Pamela Jorge. May I call you Kathleen?"

"Please, doctor, call me Kat. Everyone does."

"And you must call me Pamela," the psychologist responded as she led Kat into another room. "I like to be informal with my clients. Can I get you some herbal tea? I'd offer you coffee, but stimulants aren't conducive to what we want to accomplish today."

"Tea is fine."

Kat was directed to a comfortable-looking recliner. The treatment area, as Kat thought of the space, was large, but with the same ambience of calm tranquility that existed in the outer office. Her chair, with its back to the door, was part of a small conversation area. Pamela seated herself on a small loveseat across from Kat. She thought she heard Detective Turner come into the room but couldn't be certain because Pamela was explaining to her what she could expect from hypnosis.

"You'll never be unconscious. You'll be relaxed but completely awake and aware of our conversation. If at any time I ask something which makes you uncomfortable, please let me know."

Kat sipped her tea and nodded her acquiescence.

"Kat, do I have your permission to record this session?"

Kat started to nod again, but Pamela interrupted her. "Please respond verbally for the record."

"Yes, you may record the session," Kat said stiffly.

"And do I have your permission for Detective

Turner and the recording technician to be present during this interview?"

"Yes, of course."

Pamela encouraged her to recline the chair until she was comfortable. She also turned on some soft, relaxing music. She took Kat's tea cup, which she placed on a nearby table, and suggested that Kat close her eyes if she felt safe.

"Kat, do you know why you are here?"

"You're going to help me remember what happened on the night of the burglary."

Pamela led her through a series of suggestions to help Kat relax. Then she asked questions designed to let Kat relate the details she remembered from that night. She had come to the part of the story about stepping into the back area of the clinic, smelling the warm bodies of small animals, then the scent of something foreign—a spicy odor that didn't belong in a veterinary clinic.

"What does the smell remind you of?" Pamela asked.

"Easter dinner," Kat replied without pause.

"Easter dinner, not Easter Sunday? Tell me about Easter dinner."

"We always went to Grandma Kate's for Easter dinner. She was my mother's mother. I was named for her. She fixed a big ham scored and pierced with cloves—*cloves!* That's what I smelled the night of the break-in." Kat sat up straight.

Pamela continued in a soothing voice. "Good, you remember the smell of cloves, but don't get too excited. We want to continue through the entire episode and see what else you might remember."

Kat settled back into the recliner and tried to return to her previous relaxed state. The music helped. As she talked about stepping into the back area, she remembered feeling spooked, being chilled and thinking the back door was ajar.

"Your subconscious was aware things were not as they should be," Pamela commented. "Tell me about approaching the pharmacy."

When Kat got to the point of sticking her head inside the door, Pamela told her to stop. "You're looking into the pharmacy—what do you see?"

"There's someone—I can't see the face—bent down with his back to me and he has something over his head. He looks as if he's searching for something."

"Is the man you see Dr. Walker?"

"I can't tell." Kat shook her head. "He's

hunched over."

"Are you certain the person is a man?"

"No."

"Where is he in the pharmacy?" Pamela asked.

"He's at the far end, away from me. He has a Maglite—oh, the pharmacy lights weren't on—the light I saw was from the Maglite."

"You're doing well, Kat. We're almost at the end. Can you continue?"

"He comes at me. He's big, much bigger than Dr. Walker. The light goes out. I feel as if I'm being tackled by a linebacker. I think he hit me with the flashlight."

Kat paused for a breath, searching her memory. "I don't remember anything else until I came to. Then I had a horrible headache and, at first, I didn't know where I was."

"Kat, you will become fully conscious in the here and now. You will be aware of our session and all you remembered. You will feel rested and alert with a sense of well-being."

Kat opened her eyes, sat up, and stretched before bringing the recliner to the upright position.

Pamela congratulated her. "You did very well. Don't you agree, Detective Turner?"

"I do," Turner said. "You've provided

additional information that should help us move forward on this case."

Turner directed his attention to Dr. Jorge. "May I ask Kat a question?"

"That's for Kat to decide," Pamela said.

"Sure, detective, go ahead," Kat prompted.

"Are you certain the flashlight was a Maglite?"

"I can't say for sure. I didn't see a manufacturer's logo, if that's what you mean. But the flashlight certainly looked like one—big, long, and heavy."

Kat continued, "Detective Turner, the intruder was at the far end of the pharmacy, nowhere near the drawer with the tranquilizer darts. Were the darts a diversion?"

"There's always that possibility, Ms. Morelli, but it's not your job to solve the crime. You just leave that to me and my department."

JORDAN HAD BEEN WAITING IN the reception area for less than ten minutes when Kat and Detective Turner were escorted from the private office by the psychologist.

"Is she okay?" Jordan asked.

"She's fine," Pamela replied. "She was only in a light trance."

"May we go now?" Kat snapped.

"Sure." Jordan was a bit surprised at her abrupt interruption.

She stood stiffly as he helped her on with her coat. Then, turning to the psychologist, Kat smiled warmly. "Thank you, Pamela, for helping me to remember."

Jordan interpreted that cold to him and warm to Pamela Jorge meant he was in the doghouse for some reason.

When they reached the car, Jordan suggested they stop for lunch on their way back to Spruce Creek. Kat agreed tersely, and then sat in silence as they drove west on I-70.

When they exited onto Highway 58, she finally stirred. "Where are we going?"

"Golden," Jordan replied.

"Isn't that out of the way?"

"We're not in any hurry, and I thought that, after this morning's ordeal, a leisurely lunch in quiet surroundings would allow you to unwind. You seem stressed."

"If I am, my stress has nothing to do with the hypnosis. Why didn't you ask *me* if I was okay?"

"I did." Jordan was confused by her question.

"No, you asked Pamela. You talk about me, but you don't talk *to* me. I'd like to know why."

Jordan was suddenly uncomfortable. Kat was right. He was keeping her at arm's length. He didn't talk to her about anything personal if he could avoid it.

She was becoming an individual to him—a person with ideas and feelings, with identifiable traits. Somehow, she was insinuating herself into his life without even trying, becoming someone he might trust. He was unable to keep her in that broad category labeled *women*. That scared the hell out of him.

He did not want to be attracted to her. If he were totally honest with himself, he was afraid of her and what she might mean to him. If he let her become important in his life, she would be able to hurt him as his mother had.

"Never mind," Kat said sharply, interrupting his train of thought. "I don't expect you to answer me."

"I wasn't ignoring you—I was trying to find an answer to your question. I'm afraid I don't have one I can give you. I'll try to do better in the future."

Nestled in the foothills west of Denver, the town of Golden was the site of the original Coors Brewery and the home of the Colorado School of Mines. With a permanent population of less than twenty thousand, Golden seemed an unlikely home to one of the finest restaurants in Colorado. But the Briarwood Inn, renowned for fine food and elegant décor, enjoyed success as a result of its proximity to Denver and a reputation for hosting idyllic weddings.

When they entered the restaurant, the transition from bright Colorado sun to warm low light provided by sparkling chandeliers hanging from high ceilings was one from the bustle of modern industrial America to the ambiance of an old-world country inn. Jordan watched Kat's face as she absorbed her surroundings—stained glass reflected off dark wood, plush elegant seating, and unique antique furnishings.

When the hostess seated them in a small, intimate booth, Kat's mouth widened into a dazzling smile. "Oh, Jordan, this is exquisite. How did you ever find this place?"

"The first time I came was for a fraternity brother's wedding. But I've been back many times since."

"If the food is as good as the atmosphere, I can see why," Kat added, glancing up from the menu. "But wow, it's awfully expensive."

"That's one of the reasons I don't eat here every day—that, and the fact that it's an hour's drive from Spruce Creek."

"I bet not everything's organic," Kat teased.

"No, but much of the food is."

Jordan was amazed at Kat's ability to go from being spitting angry at him one moment to being a pleasant dining companion the next. It was one of the best things about her sunny personality—she never stayed angry for long.

Over lunch at the Briarwood, Jordan relaxed and they discussed what they found satisfying in their lives and what they would change if they could. Lunch was like a first date, when two people were just getting to know each other.

"How do you like living in Spruce Creek?" Jordan asked as they sipped iced tea.

"It's great. I like the clean mountain air. And once people learn you're not a tourist, they are very friendly."

"That's true—we aren't crazy about tourist invasions," he said with a smile. "Wait until spring—you'll find out why."

"What about you?" Kat asked, warmth in her voice. "You must like Spruce Creek since you returned there to hang out your shingle."

"You're right—going away to college introduced me to things I can do without." Jordan stretched out his hand as if he was asking

Kat to agree with him. "I don't like the hordes of people. Boulder was like an anthill. And looking down from the Flatirons, Denver air looks filthy. You must have noticed it while we were there today."

He was surprised when he found himself sharing his feelings with Kat. Slowly but surely, she was breaching his defenses.

Jordan admired Kat's openness, her ability to speak her mind and live in the moment. She had transitioned instantly from being annoyed with him to being excited about their surroundings. She wasn't coy or pseudo-sophisticated. She didn't pretend either ignorance or intellect; she openly declared what she liked and what she disliked. There was no guile in her. The only thing Kat kept off-limits was her relationship with her family. Whenever Jordan tried to steer the discussion in that direction, she pointedly changed the subject.

After lunch, they began the return drive to Spruce Creek by continuing west toward the community of Georgetown. "I'm of a mind to go home over Guanella Pass. The trip will be slower, but soon the pass will be closed until next summer. The route is a great way to see the changing of the aspen. We might as well enjoy the scenery now while we can."

"Oh, I'd love that," Kat said. "I've never been over the pass. My body took long enough to acclimate to Spruce Creek."

"The summit is over eleven thousand feet. Will that be a problem?"

"Not as long as you don't expect me to do anything more strenuous than inhale and exhale."

"Then just sit back and breathe easy," Jordan said with a grin. "Are you free to talk about the hypnosis session? Or did Turner tell you to keep the information to yourself?"

"He didn't, but even if he had, I would tell you what we discovered. You have every right to know."

Kat related what they had learned as a result of the session. When she mentioned identifying the elusive smell as cloves, the discovery teased a memory from Jordan. He would talk to Torrey about the scent of cloves. He thought perhaps they once had an employee who smoked clove cigarettes. Torrey would know.

As they continued the trip toward the summit, Jordan watched Kat enjoy swaths of quaking, shimmering aspen leaves creating golden waves along the mountainsides.

When they came abreast with the Forest

Service campground, Kat asked "Did you and your family camp here when you were a kid?"

He shook his head sadly, remembering with regret that he, his father, and his siblings had never taken any family trips. He had noticed that, in other families, it was the mothers who planned the picnics, birthday parties, and vacation trips. Without a mother, the Walkers never did any of those things.

THAT EVENING, JEREMY JOINED KAT and Jordan for dinner. He claimed it was because he wanted to find out what the hypnosis had revealed, but Kat suspected he just enjoyed a home-cooked meal and the companionship of family. He didn't have much to say and left early.

After the kitchen was cleaned and Jeremy departed, Kat settled into a big overstuffed chair in front of the fire Jordan had built to ward off the autumn chill. Reaching for her book, she glanced up to see Jordan staring.

"What? Why are you looking at me so intently?"

"I enjoy looking at you," he replied with a shrug. "Do you mind?"

Kat felt slightly breathless, and her condition

had nothing to do with altitude. "I'm not sure. You've never paid attention to me before this."

"Oh, I've paid attention to you—you just never caught me at it," he said grinning.

"Jordan, what's going on?" she asked, her voice shaky. She knew she sounded nervous. She *was* nervous.

Jordan took a deep breath before speaking "Kat, I'm attracted to you," he said hesitantly "Attracted in a way I haven't been before—not tc another woman, I mean. What I'm trying to say is, I'm comfortable with you. Your presence relaxes me."

"Oh, well, then I guess I'm safe," she said with a chuckle. "If I excited you, I might be in danger. But if I make you comfortable and relaxed, I'm in as much danger as an old slipper."

"I am not explaining this well," Jordan said, shaking his head. "Let me try this again. I like you. I'd like to get to know you better, but you work for me, and you look like a cute teenager. You're sharing my home, and I don't want to take unfair advantage, or for you to feel coerced in any way."

"Jordan, I'm twenty-six years old," Kat said, setting her book on the table and looking straight into Jordan's eyes. "I don't know how old I'll be before I stop looking like a freckle-faced teen, but I am *not* a kid, and any advantage I allow you will not be unfair. Now, what do you want to know about me that you don't know already?"

"Why won't you talk about your family?"

"Probably for the same reason you don't talk about your mother. Talking about my family is painful. I sound like a spoiled brat when I start listing my gripes about my parents and my brother."

"Tell me," he urged. "I promise I won't think of you as a spoiled brat. You *do* know that lancing a boil, while painful, lets the poison out."

"I'll talk, but I'll stop when you start snoring."

"Okay, we have a deal."

"I was born and raised in Fort Morgan, a small community halfway to Nebraska and with much the same flat, prairie atmosphere. My parents are both school teachers. They're bright, intelligent people—not geniuses, but smart and driven to succeed. I have a brother, Antonio, two years older, who is the model child. He carried a 4.0 throughout high school, was valedictorian, and got a free ride to the University of Colorado at Boulder. He now has his masters and is working on his Ph.D. at UCCS. He's handsome, charming, and everything I'm not." Kat sighed.

"I, on the other hand, am exceedingly mediocre. I received my B.S. with a 3.1 average. I didn't qualify for a scholarship, so I couldn't pursue my dream of becoming a vet. That's why I'm just a lowly vet tech."

Jordan reached over and took her hand in his. "I don't know where our relationship is headed. I may have too many scars to ever be anything more than your friend, but I *do* know that you are not mediocre. You're vibrant and alive, and you have a special talent for prodding me when I need to be prodded." He rose and pulled her into a hug. "So tell me your gripes and why you wouldn't let me contact your family when you were injured."

Kat moved out of Jordan's embrace and began to pace, wearing a path in front of the fireplace. "My gripes—okay, let's see. Nothing I do is ever good enough. I graduated college with a solid B average, but Tony finished with a 4.0 just like he did in high school, and he went on to do post-grad work. When I was in high school, I competed in gymkhana and I won blue ribbons. Tony was quarterback and captain of the winning high school football team. I was a junior rodeo queen, but Tony was homecoming king. The only competitive sport I've ever been better at than

Tony is western riding. But my parents don't think that's significant."

"Okay, but why not let them know you were hurt? Surely they would have wanted to come and see for themselves how serious your injuries were and to offer their support."

Kat shook her head. "My parents don't know where I am. If they did, they would find themselves required to meddle in my life—try to make me a better person. Well, I'm happy with the person I am—at least, as long as I am not anywhere near them. They destroy my self-esteem. They don't mean to. They're not malicious. They just spend all their time saying I should be more like my brother."

Jordan frowned. "If they don't know where you are, they must be worried sick."

"I call them at least once a week on a prepaid cell phone. That way there's no number to trace. I wouldn't put that past them, even though they know I want to be on my own. I just let them know I'm well, that I'm working in my chosen field, and that I'm happy." Kat moved to stand directly in front of Jordan. "Satisfied?"

"I am," he answered with a sigh.

"Okay, Dr. Walker, it's your turn now. Tell me about your mother."

"Not tonight, sunshine," he said and turned away. "I have a hard day ahead of me tomorrow inoculating goats. In fact, I think I'll take you with me, since you know your way around livestock."

TEN

The moment she arrived at the clinic on Friday Torrey asked Kat, "What have you done with Dr. Jordan Walker? Who is this doppelganger who has replaced him?"

"What are you talking about?" Kat laughed at her friend's silliness.

"Jordan walked into the clinic this morning with a big smile on his face. I haven't seen a smile that big since he was twelve years old, and certainly not first thing in the morning. What have you done to him?"

"Nothing," Kat answered with a shrug. "I've done nothing."

"You must have done something. He's a changed man. What did you two do yesterday? Neither of you came into the clinic."

"Jordan drove me to Denver to the psychologist, and I was able to remember some additional details. Maybe he's happy because I remembered my attacker was much bigger than him, so he couldn't possibly be the guilty party. Maybe that's why he's in a good mood."

Kat watched the office manager raise a brow, and eye her skeptically. Then Torrey said, "It has to be more than that. He was never seriously concerned about being a suspect. He knew he was innocent. So, what else happened?"

"I argued with him because he talks about me to other people as if I'm not there. I don't like that, and I let him know it."

"What else?"

"We went to lunch in Golden at the Briarwood Inn, and then we drove back from Georgetown over Guanella Pass. Then Jeremy came for dinner. I think that about covers it."

Kat didn't think the rest of it was any of Torrey's business—the fact they'd talked about being more than friends, and that he'd held her close. Those were special memories she had no intention of sharing. But secretly, she hoped that the interlude the evening before was the cause of his good mood.

"We talked a little about my background," she

offered instead. "He seemed pleased that I have experience with livestock. He said that today he wanted me to come with him to inoculate goats."

As if he'd been cued, Jordan walked into the clinic. "Torrey, I need you to outfit Kat to come with me to Whitaker's to inoculate his goats for sore mouth. Find rubber boots and heavy-duty rubber gloves to fit her." He turned to Kat. "Dress warm, long sleeves and long pants, and layers. The weather has really turned cold. I have a poncho you can wear if we get snow. Can you be ready in thirty minutes?" he asked, clearly impatient to be on his way.

"Sure. After I dress, I'll swing through the clinic and pick up the gear from Torrey. Then I'll meet you in the garage."

"Okay, let's do it," he said with a nod.

Jordan left in one direction and Torrey in another. Kat trotted up the stairs to the apartment, noting the sky was a brittle blue with dark clouds building in the west.

She stripped naked and pulled on long silk undergarments that hugged her every curve like a second skin, leaving nothing to the imagination. Pity she couldn't show off for Jordan, she thought. She'd bet he'd never seen long underwear like hers. She couldn't help but blush at the naughty thoughts.

She covered her sexy lingerie with a lightweight turtleneck and blue jeans. Then she slid into a flannel shirt and sturdy hiking boots. After braiding her hair tightly so it wouldn't fall in her face, she was ready for anything.

Kat swung through the clinic to pick up the gear that Torrey had assembled for her, and then headed for the garage.

Jordan had finished loading the medical supplies and was waiting for her. He pushed a step stool in front of the open passenger door and helped her up into the SUV.

When they were on their way, the wind buffeted the truck and sneaked through the cracks, making Kat grateful she had dressed as she had.

"So," Jordan said as she watched the wintery landscape go by, "what do you know about sore mouth and the inoculation for it?"

Kat didn't take offense at his questioning her education. She knew he was asking so he would be certain she could work safely. "I know that you wouldn't be inoculating unless there is now, or has been in the past, an outbreak of the disease. I know the vaccine is live virus and very infectious to humans, which is why we use rubber boots and heavy-duty rubber gloves. I know that you are doing the inoculations now so that the kids born in spring will have immunity through their mothers. Have I left anything out?"

"Is that all textbook learning, or have you done this in the past?"

"It's textbook. I've been fortunate never to have come in contact with this particular disease."

"In that case, I'll do the first few so you can watch and learn. Then you'll do a few under my supervision so I can watch your technique. When I'm satisfied, we'll both perform inoculations. Whitaker has two chutes, so his hands can split the herd. He has approximately two hundred goats all together."

"Why so many goats?"

"He rents them out for grassland management. It doesn't take too many goats to reduce the danger of grass fires. Matt has a lot of customers with high-country properties. They keep a goat or two around their summer cabins for the season. The practice is cheap, efficient, and ecologically sound."

"Does that produce enough income to sustain his ranch?"

"No, but the goats don't need to support him. Matt is well off. He owns a large and successful construction company in Denver. He dabbles in other things from time to time. He might be a gentleman rancher, but he's not afraid to get his hands dirty."

Jordan turned the four-wheel drive vehicle off the well-maintained gravel road onto a rutted track that wound through a thick spruce forest. All around, sunlight darted through tree branches littering the shadowed road with bright splotches of brilliance. The continuous transition from shadow to bright light made it difficult to focus.

Kat was glad that Jordan was driving slowly when a deer broke through the underbrush and dashed across the road immediately in front of the bumper. Jordan braked hard, and Kat was thrown into her seatbelt.

"Are you okay?" he asked.

"I'm fine, just a little shaken. How's the deer?"

"Long gone—she didn't even pause."

"Well, I'm glad no one was hurt. Are there a lot of deer that we need to look out for?"

"You probably won't see another deer in the high-country between now and Thanksgiving. Hunting season will be starting soon. Then we'll need to look out for armed hunters instead of unarmed deer."

JORDAN PARKED THE SUV IN front of an impressive ranch house built of spruce logs separated from a native stone patio by a generous porch. Large picture windows looked out on colorful planters hosting monkshood. Fall crocus spread around the front of the house, coloring the landscape with swaths of lavender, purple, and violet. Jordan thought again how foolish his sister had been to run away from all this.

As Jordan and Kat climbed out of the truck, Matt Whitaker strode down the steps from the porch and embraced Jordan in a big man-hug.

As soon as Matt released him, Jordan pulled Kat forward to introduce her. "Kat, this is Matthew Whitaker, my brother-in-law. Matt, this is Kat Morelli, my primary veterinary technician."

"It's a pleasure to meet you, Mr. Whitaker. Jordan never mentioned that you were related."

"If my wife doesn't come home soon, I may become his ex-brother-in-law."

Jordan shook his head as if to warn *don't ask*. Then he suggested they get to work.

"The goats are in the lower pasture," Matt said as he climbed into the back seat of the SUV.

Knowing how difficult it was for Kat to climb into the oversized vehicle, Jordan put his hands on her waist and lifted her into the seat.

"Damn it, Jordan, you're treating me like a pet again. I can get into the truck without being lifted in."

Matt grinned. "For a little thing, your Kat sure has sharp claws."

Kat scowled. "Don't encourage him, Mr. Whitaker."

"Gotcha. Since we're certain to be working together, you should call me Matt."

Jordan thought it best that he not add fuel to the fire, so he kept his mouth shut and steered the vehicle down a dirt track to the lower pasture. He stopped between two large pens, one empty and one filled with bleating goats.

Jordan asked Matt to have his hands set the chutes widely spaced at either end of the parked SUV so both he and Kat would have equal access to the supplies.

"Matt, I want you outside the chutes, and remind your crew that no one is to touch any of the inoculated goats without gloves until the scabs have healed over. Also, the goats are not to mingle with other livestock."

While Matt was talking to his men and reminding them of the safety procedures required, Jordan and Kat donned protective gear and prepared to begin the inoculations.

The first goat was shoved into the chute. Jordan grabbed its ear and scraped the inside flesh, then applied the vaccine. The goat was then pushed through the gate in the chute into the empty paddock. As soon as the gate dropped behind the vaccinated goat, a new one appeared in the chute. Jordon performed the same procedure again.

When he was done, he looked at Kat. "Think you can do this?" he asked.

"Let's find out." Her eyes sparkled brightly with the challenge.

Just as she'd seen Jordan do, she grabbed the ear of the goat in the chute, scraped the inside surface, applied the vaccine, and shoved the animal through the forward gate. The next animal was bleating in front of her, and she repeated the procedure.

Jordan grabbed a package of vaccine ampoules and moved to the other chute. "With both of us working, we should be able to finish in a couple of hours. But take a break when you need to. And whatever you do, don't push your hair out of your face when you have your gloves on."

Kat nodded acknowledgement and grabbed a goat's ear.

They both worked steadily, the only sounds the bleating of goats and the dropping of gates at either end of the chutes. Jordan heaved a sigh of relief when he realized that the number of vaccinated goats greatly outnumbered those which had yet to be done. He'd like to take a break, but Kat hadn't slowed down, so he wasn't about to.

When the gate had fallen behind the last goat, he met Kat at the SUV. They deposited the used supplies in biohazard bags. Knowing the size of the herd, Jordan hadn't brought much in the way of extra vaccines, so the few remaining were deposited with the used ampoules in the same bags as were the rubber gloves. All would be incinerated. Better to destroy a few viable inoculations than have live vaccine in the clinic.

"I'd like it if you two could stay for lunch," Matt said as the chutes were pulled away and he came toward the SUV.

Jordan paused, remembering Kat's complaints about being treated like a pet instead of a person. "Thanks, Matt, I'd like that. But you'd best ask Kat herself. I don't want to speak for the both of us. "

"Thank you, Matt, we'd love to stay. But we don't want to cause you any extra work."

"No extra work—Consuela will love entertaining someone other than me."

Jordan saw Kat's raised eyebrows and mouthed *housekeeper*.

Matt hopped in the back seat and Jordan followed Kat to the passenger side, but he didn't touch her. He watched her struggle to get her foot up on the high running board and then stretch to reach the grab-handle above her head. She couldn't quite touch it.

She snorted in frustration. "Okay, Dr. Walker, I guess I *do* need your assistance to get into the SUV. I'm going to carry a step stool in the future."

Jordan grinned. Turning her to face him, he wrapped his hands around her waist and lifted her into the truck.

As he drove slowly back up the hill to the ranch house, he pondered why he enjoyed having an excuse to put his hands on Kat.

ELEVEN

When they returned to Spruce Creek and drove into the yard behind the clinic, Kat could only think of how much she longed for a shower. She smelled of goat, and she didn't believe Jordan would object if she skipped going back into the clinic and opted to drag herself up the stairs to the apartment. But in all fairness to Jordan, before she looked to her own comfort, she needed to help empty the SUV and get the bio-waste into the incinerator.

Jordan came around the front and opened her door while she pulled on a new pair of rubber gloves. He helped her from the truck and they started for the rear when Kat stopped dead in her tracks and groaned. "Oh, no. It can't be."

"Is something wrong?"

"That inappropriately well-dressed couple headed this direction—they're my parents."

"Are you upset because they look as if they should be having lunch at the Brown Palace instead of walking across a gravel parking lot in the Colorado high country?"

"No, I'm upset because they're here. How in hell did they find me?"

"We're about to find out," Jordan remarked, straightening to his full height.

Kat watched Jordan step forward to intercept her parents. "Mr. & Mrs. Morelli, I'm Dr. Jordan Walker. I look forward to getting to know you, but I must ask you to step away from us. We've just come from inoculating a herd of goats, and we need to dispose of hazardous waste and disinfect before we come in contact with anyone."

Kat looked at Jordan. She knew he was exaggerating, because they'd eaten lunch with Matt Whitaker. She raised her eyebrows when he continued. "Please make yourself at home in our apartment. It's at the top of the stairs above the clinic. The door is unlocked."

Her parents looked taken aback but agreed, then turned and started up the stairs.

"Jordan," Kat whispered harshly, "what did

you mean by *our* apartment? It's *your* apartment."

"Last I checked, we're roommates. So it is *our* apartment."

She rolled her eyes. "But you know what my parents are going to think."

"Do you mind? You're a grown-up—you have the right to live your life as you see fit. I thought that was the reason you left home and migrated to the high country."

He took her gloved hand and led her to the tailgate of the SUV. They unloaded the supplies and took the bio-bags to the incinerator. After being turned to ash, the vaccine was no longer viable or dangerous. They disposed of their protective gear and washed in the deep sink in the garage.

As they climbed the stairs, Jordan chatted casually about the Whitaker ranch, diverting her attention from the confrontation she feared. She expected that her parents would hear the conversation. She hoped they would interpret it as a normal boss/employee dialogue.

When they walked into the apartment, Jordan continued talking. "Kat, why don't you take the first shower, then you and your folks can visit while I clean up. I'll call Torrey and tell her we're both available if she needs us, but that we have no plans to return to the clinic today unless necessary."

With a nod, Kat fled to her room, leaving the door open a crack so she could eavesdrop. Her father took the lead. "Dr. Walker, what is going on between you and my daughter?"

Kat could just imagine the scowl on his face.

"Please, call me Jordan. In answer to your question, nothing is going on between Kat and me. She's my employee, and my roommate. That's all."

"Why is she your roommate?" her father demanded. "That's an unusual arrangement for a boss and an employee, wouldn't you say?"

Kat held her breath. She didn't want Jordan to tell them why she was living with him.

"Perhaps it's unusual in Fort Morgan, but in the high country employees frequently live on site. When Kat first came to Spruce Creek, she was living in a small duplex apartment on the far side of town—not at all practical. She's my primary veterinary technician, very important to my practice. I can't afford to have her stranded on the other side of town during a blizzard, or freezing to death because the utilities fail."

Kat relaxed. Jordan was covering for her. She grabbed her robe and headed for the bathroom, convinced that her parents could have no objection to her living arrangements.

Still, she couldn't help but wonder when she'd been promoted to his *primary veterinary technician*. Hadn't he said the same to Matt Whitaker this afternoon? Apparently, she was *very important to his practice*. She'd have to ask him about that later.

She showered quickly, leaving Jordan plenty of hot water, then wrapped her hair in a towel and hurried back to her room.

When she joined her parents in the living room, she was comfortably dressed in black leggings and a wool ski sweater, and her hair was in a single braid. Jordan had started a fire, and she curled into her favorite chair nearby. She was warm and clean. Had her family not been there, she would be stretched out on her bed taking a nap.

Ignoring her parents for a moment, she directed her attention to Jordan. "I left you plenty of hot water, boss," she said as he rose to leave. She knew if they'd been alone, he would have made a comment about her calling him *boss*; she could see him restrain himself. Maybe she was coming to understand him a little bit.

As soon as Jordan left the room, she faced her parents. "So, how did you find me, and why are you here?"

"Tony found you," her mother replied. "He started calling animal clinics and asking for you by name. Yesterday, he called here and was told that you were out but expected back later in the day. So," she spread her arms wide, "here we are."

Kat stared hard at her parents, barely able to believe what she was hearing. *Did they think she was incapable?*

"The *why* is very simple," her father continued. "We were worried about you. And with good cause, it would seem, since we've found you living with a man."

TWELVE

J ordan and Kat lingered over breakfast, talking about her parents. Since it was Saturday, they had no scheduled clinic hours, even if they were on call. The service knew they were available, so there was no need to rush.

"Did your parents drive back to Fort Morgan last night?" Jordan asked.

"No, they're staying at a B&B in Grant. They plan on being here all weekend. Tony is driving up today to join them. What is it called when a group of people decide to interfere in your life—an intervention? I think they're planning an intervention."

"Kat, they're here because they love you. They want what they believe is best for you."

"They want me to return home to Fort

Morgan.   I. AM. NOT. GOING. BACK!" With that, Kat jumped up and started clearing the table.

Jordan knew she needed movement to burn off her frustration. He hoped the dishes would weather the storm that was brewing in his kitchen.

When it appeared that the worst of Kat's temper had calmed, Jordan suggested inviting her family for dinner that evening. Kat objected. He pointed out that seeing her in a safe and secure environment, seeing that they weren't *living* together but that they were simply roommates, would assure them of her wellbeing.

Kat acquiesced grudgingly and fled the kitchen. When she returned, she was dressed for outdoors.

"Where are you going?" Jordan asked.

"I'm going to clean the dog pens and check on the strays we're holding."

"That's not your job."

"I know, but I like spending time with the dogs. They accept me for who I am—they don't try to change me."

Jordan watched her back, ramrod straight, as she descended the stairs.

He puttered around the kitchen, thinking about what he would serve for dinner. They would eat in the dining room. Kat would get a kick out of that. He would invite Jeremy. His brother would probably show up anyway, but if he received an invitation, maybe he might dress better.

A knock at the door interrupted his musings. He was not surprised to find the Morelli family on the landing.

"Good morning. Come in," he invited.

"Where's Kathleen?" Kat's father demanded. He was a swarthy man, good-looking for his age, his Italian heritage obvious.

Ignoring the older man's rude behavior, Jordan held out his hand to a younger version of Kat's father. "Hello, you must be Tony. I'm Jordan Walker. Welcome to my home."

Tony Morelli exchanged a firm handshake with Jordan. "Thank you. It's a pleasure to meet you. Is my sister here?"

"No, she's working in the kennels. She enjoys spending time with the dogs. She tells me it's because they accept her without trying to change her."

"Do you try to change her?" Tony asked.

"No, I like Kat just the way she is—I wouldn't dream of trying to change her. It would be a wasted effort, in any case. She isn't going to change for anyone."

Tony nodded. The two men understood each other.

Jordan ushered Kat's family into the living room, offered them coffee, and then called Kat's cell. "Your family's here. You should come back."

"I'm on my way," she said, resignation in her voice.

When she could be heard climbing the stairs, Kat's parents gathered at the door to welcome her. She came in with a red nose and wind-watery eyes and carrying muddy boots in her hands.

"It's getting blustery out there. We're in for snow, and soon. I turned the heat up in the kennels," she told Jordan.

She patted her eyes dry with a tissue that Jordan handed her. When she was able to see clearly, she greeted her family. She hugged her brother. It was obvious to Jordan that, no matter how much she complained about Tony's perceived perfection and her parents' supposed preference for him, the two siblings were close.

Jordan picked up where Kat had left off. "We haven't had a serious storm yet this season. We've had snow, of course—this is the high country— but a freezing blizzard before Halloween isn't uncommon." He glanced at Kat's father and brother. "You both have all-wheel drive and chains, don't you?"

Tony nodded.

"I have snow tires," Mr. Morelli said.

"That may not be enough, Mr. Morelli. But we'll make certain you don't get stranded."

Tony spoke up. "Jordan, my father's name is Emilio and my mother's name is Bridget. They're Mr. and Mrs. Morelli only in the classroom."

Emilio Morelli hung his head in embarrassment. "My son is right. You've been gracious to us, and we owe you similar courtesy."

Jordan could see Kat breathe a sigh of relief. Apparently, a dam had been breached. A flood of understanding swept over Jordan as he realized that Kat had feared her family would reject him.

Tony was his father's son—tall with dark hair, olive skin, and old-world charm. Like Kat, Bridget Morelli had luxuriant, ginger hair. He guessed that she also shared her daughter's fiery temper and a sharp tongue. The two women moved down the hall to Kat's room and the men settled in front of the fire in the living room.

"I must ask you again, Jordan, what are your intentions toward my daughter?" The question was rendered in a calm, respectful voice—a big change from the previous day.

"I don't know that I can answer you. My intentions are dependent upon Kat's wishes. I care for her." Jordan shifted uncomfortably in his chair. "She's bright, intelligent, and hardworking. She's a good friend and a valued employee. There is no other relationship between us at this time."

Tony grinned at him. "My father has you on the hot seat, like a recalcitrant student. He's good at it. I should know—I grew up with him as my interrogator."

"I'd like to know her better, but that must be her choice," Jordan concluded, grateful for Tony's friendly comment. "We must all wait and see—even you, Emilio."

When, by mid afternoon, the skies had darkened significantly, Jordan encouraged Tony to move his Subaru Outback into the clinic's oversized garage. He ran a rope line from the stairs to the garage so that even in a whiteout they could move safely between the two locations. He confirmed that there was plenty of fuel for the generators that would light both the clinic and the apartment if Public Service Company lost power, which Jordan expected. He and Tony both carried additional wood up to the apartment and stacked it by the fireplace.

"We're as ready as we can be," Jordan spoke to the room at large. "I sent my employees home. I phoned my brother and asked him to join us for dinner. I suggested he come early, before the storm moves in. There's nothing else to do."

"We're no strangers to blizzards," Bridget remarked. "We get at least one each winter out on the plains. We just hunker down, play poker, and drink Irish coffee."

"Sounds like a plan to me," Jordan said with an easy laugh.

When Jeremy arrived, Jordan went through introductions. When asked if he and Jeremy were the only siblings, he explained that they had a sister who was back east.

Later, the four men settled in front of the TV, beer in hand, to watch the Colorado Rams host the Hawaii Warriors in a Mountain West Conference meet. Jordan wasn't a big college football fan, but CSU was his alma mater so he paid lip service to being a team supporter. At half-time he put a leg of lamb in the oven.

WHILE THE MEN WATCHED FOOTBALL, Kat and Bridget settled in the kitchen. They talked about a variety of things. Kat could tell her mother really was interested in what she did at the clinic. So, she explained her job duties and how they had changed in the time since she began working for Jordan.

She embarrassedly admitted that her hot-tempered tongue had gotten away from her and she had *lectured* him—his word, she explained—about not having a senior discount.

"I love working with the animals. We see mostly cats and dogs, but we occasionally make house calls and go out to a rancher's site. That's where we were yesterday, inoculating goats."

Kat was brimming with confidence and she knew she was exhibiting her elevated self-esteem to her mother. However, she admitted to herself, all was not perfect. Dr. Jordan Walker thought of her as an immature young woman, and she was determined to open his eyes.

"So, are you interested in him?" her mother asked.

"Absolutely."

"Is he interested in you?"

"I think so," Kat replied. "But he thinks that since we're roommates and he's my boss, that he would be taking advantage of me if he showed that interest."

"Well then, Kathleen Bridget Morelli, if you

want him, you must trap him."

"Mom!" Kat stared at her mother wide-eyed.

"Hush." She waved one hand in dismissal. "We have never had this particular mother/daughter talk. I am not suggesting you get pregnant or anything like that. But if you make him happy and comfortable with you in his life, he won't be able to consider life without you. You'll be simply irresistible."

Bridget motioned for Kat to come closer. "This is what I had to do with your father. He, too, is an honorable man, and they are the worst kind. This is what you must do . . ."

Heads together and giggling, they didn't notice when Jordan entered to check the lamb.

"What are you two ladies up to?" he asked teasingly.

Their heads popped up, and Kat knew she must be as red-faced and guilty looking as her mother. "Just girl talk," she said brightly.

"Well, how about setting the dining room table for dinner? Oh, and open a couple bottles of Jack Rabbit Hill and let them breathe."

"Sure thing, boss." She threw him a saucy grin over her shoulder.

In the dining room, she pulled the heavy drapes over the windows. The snow had begun, and it was coming down heavily. In an effort to make the room warmer and more welcoming, she turned on all the lights, then set lit candles on the table and the sideboard.

Jordan was pulling the lamb from the oven when Kat heard what she thought was pounding on the door. She pulled it open to find Matt Whitaker looking like the Abominable Snowman, standing on the landing.

"Matt, get in here out of the cold. Are you okay?"

"I am now. Thank God for the rope from the garage. Without the line, I would never have made it."

Out of curiosity, everyone crowded into the kitchen. Kat introduced Matt to her family.

"I'm sorry, Kat. If I knew you and Jordan had company, I would have gone to Jessie's. I didn't mean to intrude."

"Don't be silly," Jordan said. "Jessie's place would be an ice cube. You're much better off here, and you're just in time for dinner."

Kat moved to the dining room to set another place while Jordan helped Matt peel off his ice-encrusted coat. Then Matt sat at the kitchen table and worked at getting his frosty boots off.

"Jeremy, get Matt dry socks out of my dresser

and bring him a towel," Jordan called out, then turned his attention to Matt. "What happened to you? Why are you out in this weather? I expected you would be all toasty and warm at the ranch."

"I drove Consuela to the airport in Denver. She's flying to California to visit her sister. When I started back, it was windy but clear. But the closer I got to the Front Range, the more threatening the clouds looked. The snow started before I got to Bailey, but I still wasn't worried. By the time I got to Spruce Creek, I was in white-out conditions. My truck will go anywhere, up the side of a canyon if necessary, but I have to see which way to point it. So I figured I would crash on your couch."

Kat laughed. "Well, it looks as if you boys are going to have a sleepover, or whatever it is that guys call a slumber party. Mom and Dad can have your room, Jordan, and we'll pull blankets and quilts in front of the fireplace for you guys."

Kat wondered if Jordan would resent her making the sleeping assignments, but it was only logical to have her parents take Jordan's bed and the guys to bunk in the living room. She had no intention of sending anyone on their way to the B&B in Grant.

Laughing and chatting, they settled at the

dining room table. Kat set the side dishes on the table as Jordan stood slicing the lamb and Jeremy poured the wine.

When everyone was seated, Tony said, "In our family, it's customary to offer grace before special meals. May we do that, Jordan, or will it make anyone uncomfortable?"

Kat looked toward Jordan on her right, concerned that he would, indeed, be uncomfortable. But she discerned no sense of unease.

Jordan nodded. "I think that's a lovely tradition, and God knows we have much to be grateful for tonight. So, please, go ahead."

Tony offered the grace and then asked everyone to contribute, if they were so inclined.

Matt spoke first. "I'm grateful to be warm, safe, and dry, instead of buried in a snow drift."

They went around the table, each mentioning something of importance to him or her.

Jordan went last. "I'm grateful to be seated in this dining room surrounded by family and friends, while outside a blizzard rages. It's been a long time since this room has been used, but I hope that is about to change."

After a heartfelt "Amen," plates were filled, conversation picked up, and the buzz of happy people sharing food and companionship filled the room.

Kat tapped the side of her wine glass. "I would like to propose a toast to the cook. Jordan, you have outdone yourself tonight."

There were murmurs of agreement as wine glasses were lifted to lips.

Bridget, seated across from Kat, raised her glass. "These potatoes are delicious, Jordan. I've never had scalloped potatoes that tasted quite like these. What's your secret?"

"Sage, nutmeg, and Asiago cheese. It's not difficult to make—I'll have Kat send you the recipe."

"You should all know that everything on this table is organic," Kat contributed. "Jordan feels that not only is organic food healthier, but that it tastes better, as well."

"You won't get any argument from me," Tony responded. Everyone agreed.

Kat sighed, for once all the people in her life seemed to be in harmony.

THIRTEEN

When Sunday morning arrived, Jordan groaned as he stretched and prepared to push up from the floor. Jeremy and Tony were stirring, as well. Matt, exhausted by his ordeal of driving in the blizzard, still snored quietly.

The night before, Jeremy had rummaged through Jordan's closet and dresser and found sweats and heavy socks for each of the men. They built up the fire, laid blankets on the floor to provide both cushion and insulation, climbed into bed rolls, and spent a relatively comfortable night. But the fire had died and the room was now cold.

"Jeremy, you stir up the fire and I'll start the coffee."

"What can I do to help?" Tony asked quietly.

"If you're willing, you could pick up the bed

rolls." Jordan looked out the window. "We'll need them again tonight. We have more than three feet of fresh snow and it's still coming down. The snow is not blowing as much, but it'll not be melting any time soon. And I guarantee that the county won't get the road to the highway plowed until this storm is over."

Years ago, Jordan's father had painted twelve-inch measures up the outside of the garage. Now, anyone could look out the window and see how much snow had accumulated.

Jordan moved to the kitchen to begin the promised coffee. Jeremy stirred the coals in the fireplace and added kindling and then logs.

"Where do you want me to store the bed rolls?" Tony asked.

"As soon as Kat is up we can put them in her room."

"Hey, she's my sister. I can put them in her room even if she's not up."

When Tony opened the door to Kat's room, Jordan could hear muffled protest and sibling banter. Jordan couldn't help but smile, happy that Kat had such a good relationship with her brother.

Soon Kat came into the kitchen fully dressed. "We don't have enough eggs to go around, so I'll make pancakes for breakfast. I can make enough of those to fill our stomachs. But first, I'm going to feed the dogs."

"Wait until I get my boots on and I'll go with you. I don't want you out in the storm by yourself."

Leave Kat to think of the animals first, Jordan thought to himself. She was the perfect helpmate to a high-country vet.

When they were both bundled up, they braved the stairs to the ground and across to the clinic door. Thankfully, Jordan thought, Kat had turned the heat up so the clinic didn't feel like a freezer, just a refrigerator. Three dogs were huddled inside their kennels as far from the outside access as possible.

"We'll give them extra rations; they need the calories in this cold," Jordan said. "And then since they seem disinclined to fight each other, maybe we can put them into one kennel so they can bunch up like a wolf pack and keep each other warm."

Jordan watched Kat fill buckets with tepid water. He understood that she wasn't going to give them cold water because it would just chill them on the inside, which they didn't need. After the dogs had finished eating, Jordan moved them all into one kennel. There was some sniffing but no growling or other signs of aggression. The single male established himself as pack leader, and the dogs settled down. They really did seem to appreciate being together.

Before returning to the apartment, Jordan walked through the clinic and checked the doors. Satisfied that everything was as it should be, he led Kat out the back and up the stairs to the apartment.

When they entered through the kitchen door, Jordan immediately noticed that the space was now warmed up. They peeled off their outer wear and Kat started preparations for breakfast. Everyone was up, dressed, and drinking coffee comfortably in front of the fire. Jordan walked into the living room with the pot and asked if anyone wanted refills. Emilio requested one and Jordan complied.

"Where did you and my daughter go?" Emilio asked.

"We went to take care of the dogs. They needed to be fed and watered, and I needed to be certain that the ambient temperature in the clinic was adequate. The dogs are content even when we would find the surroundings cold, but can't be confined in freezing temperature."

"And you needed her help to do this?"

"It was your daughter's idea to see to the dogs before she fixed breakfast. I went to help her and to be certain she was kept safe."

Jordan could see the surprise on Emilio's face. Bridget had a slightly smug smile on hers.

Before the conversation could continue, Kat called out from the kitchen. "Jordan, will you set the dining room table for breakfast? There's not enough space in the kitchen for seven of us."

"I'm on my way." Jordan thought how much they sounded like an old married couple. The idea didn't scare the hell out of him the way it would have some months ago.

He and Kat needed to talk.

FOURTEEN

The snow storm had ended late Sunday morning. The county plows had arrived in Spruce Creek by late afternoon and made the roads passable. Jeremy had cleared the snow from in front of the garage the old fashioned way, using a shovel. Then they were able to get the doors open. Matt drove the little Bobcat out and made quick work of clearing the parking area and the driveway.

Matt headed up to his ranch and Jeremy went wherever Jeremy went. Kat's family, however, spent one more night in Jordan's apartment.

It was with great relief that Kat saw her family depart early Monday, and she went down to work in the clinic.

When she thought about their visit, which had

not been nearly as bad as it might have been, she was grateful that they had made the effort to find her. The family appeared to like Jordan, and he had tolerated their idiosyncrasies with amazingly good grace.

One thought kept twisting in her brain—when had she gone from detesting Jordan to liking and respecting him? Then there was her mother's suggestion that she needed to *trap* Jordan into taking the next step in their relationship. She wasn't certain that she was capable of trapping him, and it didn't feel honest. She would be better off telling him the truth about how she felt about him.

They needed to talk.

Kat and Jordan went about their work, barely coming in contact with each other throughout the day. There were the usual storm-related injuries. A car had slid out of control on ice and hit Mrs. Hennessy's dog, Millie. Fortunately, the dog's hip wasn't broken, but badly bruised.

Mr. Castro's Thor had ingested chocolate. The dog was brought in to the clinic in time for them to treat the animal and save his life. But Jordan went on a rampage, impressing on Thor's owner that chocolate must be safely contained, since dogs will eat anything. Jordan could be heard throughout the entire clinic. Kat felt certain that Mr. Castro would never be so careless again.

There were far fewer cats to be treated. When the cold weather arrived, cats just curled up in a warm spot and stayed there. And, unlike dogs, they didn't eat everything in sight. Cats were far less likely to get injured or poisoned. They did see one cat that day—he had curled up too close to the fireplace and been burned by a popping ember.

Kat was pleased when the work day finally came to an end and she could retire to the apartment and put her feet up. She carefully made her way across the ice that still coated the walkway between the clinic and the apartment steps. A combination of salt and sand had been scattered on the steps so they were ice free. Nonetheless, she exercised caution climbing the stairs.

When she entered the chilly apartment, she wasted no time stirring the embers in the fireplace and adding kindling. When she had a small blaze going, she placed two thick logs in the fire chamber, hoping they would burn all night, and poured herself a glass of Jack Rabbit Hill. Pulling the big overstuffed chair closer to the fire, she relaxed for the first time that day.

She drifted into a light doze where she daydreamed that she and Jordan were a real couple and that the apartment over the clinic was her permanent home. Once again, she wished she knew how Jordan felt about her as a woman—not as a veterinary assistant, not as an intellectual sparring partner, and not as a platonic roommate.

Kat knew Jordan was reticent to discuss his mother and what her abandonment meant to him. She'd taken the requisite Psych 101 in college; she understood he probably had misplaced guilt, believing he was in some way responsible for his mother's departure. Jordan also was firmly convinced women were untrustworthy creatures by nature. She'd heard him share his opinion with Jeremy enough times to know exactly how he felt. Kat's job was to change his mind.

Her thoughts drifted to things she could improve in the apartment to make their surroundings warm and appealing—a home that Jordan would be drawn to, where he would enjoy spending time. She thought she should ask his permission before making changes. On second thought, she wouldn't ask, she'd just proceed with her plans. She had learned long ago that it's easier to receive forgiveness than to get permission.

She visualized bright, braided throw rugs scattered on the hardwood floors. She would put a large oval one in front of the fireplace, a smaller one on the side of her bed, and one in Jordan's room, too. The walls needed pictures with bright colors. Not hunting scenes—Jordan wouldn't like anything like that—but maybe cowboys or horses, chuck wagons and cattle drives. Western scenes. She would go online next weekend and search for appropriate accessories for the apartment.

Kat wouldn't ask him for a penny toward accessorizing their home. She received her full salary, but her room and board were free. She had surrendered her rental. The only expense she now had was fuel for her car, which she almost never drove, and payments on her student loans. She had been banking all the rest.

They needed a pet, as well. Who had ever heard of a vet without animals of his own? She would keep her eyes and ears open for a cat or kitten, for starters. They could move up to a family dog later.

Her mind was jumping from place to place— new curtains in the kitchen, new drapes in the dining room, new fixtures in the bathroom. But she needed to slow down. She couldn't do all these things at once. She needed to take it slowly and make subtle changes. If she tried to do everything at once, Jordan might decide to stop her.

Her mind was so focused on planning that she didn't hear Jordan come through the door. She jumped when he laid a hand on her shoulder. "I didn't hear you come in," she said breathlessly.

"I know. You were so deep in thought that you didn't even hear me when I spoke directly to you. What were you thinking about?'

"The future," Kat replied candidly.

JORDAN REALIZED THAT THIS WAS exactly the opening he wanted. They needed to talk, and there was no better time than the present.

"Kat," he began tentatively, "can we talk about the future—yours and mine?"

"Okay . . . you make it sound as if we have a future together."

"We might. Your father asked about my intentions. He sounded like someone in a Victorian romance novel."

"What did you tell him?" she asked, looking up at him curiously.

"I told him my intentions depended upon

what *you* want." Jordan walked to where the wine bottle rested and poured a glass. He was afraid to be too open. He knew that Kat could destroy him, if she chose to. He believed that she was different from other women, women like his mother, but only time would tell.

"Kat, how would you feel if our friendship moved toward an intimate relationship?" He took a sip of wine to steady him. This was possibly one of the most difficult conversations he'd ever had. He prayed he wasn't rushing their relationship too fast. "Do you have any feelings for me that aren't platonic? Please be truthful. If the answer is *no,* I would prefer to know that now."

"Jordan, what if I invest my affections and your feelings change in the future? What then?"

Jordan paced the length of the room, pushing his fingers through his hair. He felt like he was about to jump off a cliff without a parachute.

"I can't make you promises. I don't intend to marry or father any children. Can you accept that?"

Kat barely nodded.

"If we both invest our affections, if we both take a risk and find we aren't compatible, I can live with that. I want no part of a relationship, though, if this is to be only a game."

Jordan knew he had said something wrong when Kat sat up and looked at him with disgust.

"Do you really think I could enter into a relationship with you or with anyone else and treat it as a game? Is that the kind of person you think I am?" Kat spit the words out.

"No, no, I'm explaining myself poorly." Jordan knew he had to be completely honest with Kat, no matter how painful such honestly would be.

"That's not what I think. I only know I suffer with a horrible fear of opening myself to others, especially women. I *am* fond of you, but I'm a coward about entering into a relationship. Frankly, I'm terrified of being abandoned again. You have it within your power to destroy me, Kat. The fact that I'm even discussing this with you shows that I trust you. I know you won't intentionally hurt me."

Kat settled back into the chair. "I'm going to answer your questions in reverse order. Yes, I have feelings for you that aren't just platonic. I like you a lot and I would welcome your attentions, provided they include sharing some of who you are. I don't want attention from a stranger. As for the first question, intimacy would depend on us getting to truly know each other.

I'm not opposed to hugs and kisses for starters, but I don't think I'll be hopping into your bed tonight. Is that direct enough for you?"

Jordan grinned like a kid winning a foot race. "You really do speak your mind. You might just be the most truthful person I've ever known. Okay, then . . . how about we start with the hugs and kisses?" He reached for Kat's hand and pulled her into his arms. Touching his lips to hers, he tasted gently. He didn't want to frighten her away. She was important to him, and he wanted her to understand that he would never force her, or hurt her, or demand anything from her that she didn't want to give.

When he touched his tongue to her lower lip, she hesitated for a second before opening to him. Their tongues sparred tip-to-tip until he invaded her mouth. She stilled for a moment and then relaxed, letting him explore her mouth. But her hands were all over him, pushing up into his hair, sliding down his neck, pulling his shoulders to her.

He moved his hands down her back, pressing her closer. He felt her breasts pushing against his chest. Thank God he had removed his lab coat before he came up to the apartment. He could feel her heart beating through his sweater, and he felt a part of his anatomy rising to the occasion.

"Am I moving too fast?" he asked when she pushed him away, breaking the contact.

"Maybe, maybe not. But I *do* need to breathe." Her eyes were sparkling mischievously, her lips dancing with the hint of a grin.

"Breathing is a good thing. I would hate to lose you to suffocation so early in our relationship." He smiled wryly, tweaking her ear.

Jordan stepped back and took a long look at Kat. He had become accustomed to her petite stature, her ginger braids, and her freckled face. She might look like Heidi, but when she kissed him back he knew she had the heart of Boudicca, the first century Celtic warrior queen.

"Why are you looking at me that way?" Kat asked.

"What way?"

"As if you want to consume me?"

"Probably because I do—want to consume you." He cleared his throat awkwardly. "But maybe I should wait until after dinner. You can be dessert."

With that, Jordan walked into the kitchen and started rattling pots and pans. He knew he would struggle to maintain control. His body was on fire. He wanted to pull her clothes off and make her his. He wanted to see her fiery red hair unbraided and spread over his pillow. He wanted to bury his face between her breasts.

He stuck his head under the cold water tap instead.

Even if their relationship progressed the way he hoped, he couldn't be attacking her in the clinic. That kind of behavior wouldn't be professional. He didn't for a minute think he could keep their changed circumstances from being known. Torrey would know in a minute the next time she saw them together. But they must maintain a façade in their work environment.

"How about homemade pasta for dinner with Bolognese sauce?" he called out. "When I made the last batch, I froze some."

Kat walked into the kitchen. "No need to yell, I'm right here," she gently rebuked him. "Pasta sounds great. Shall I make a salad?"

"Please do." He smiled at her. "This seems so right, the two of us working in the kitchen together."

"We've been working in the kitchen together for some months now."

"I know, but this seems different somehow," Jordan said. "Does that make any sense?"

"It does make sense. We've now admitted to a

bond that we tried to ignore in the past. We're doing things as a couple now, not just two people together."

Jordan laughed and pulled Kat back into his arms. "I like being a couple," he said, nuzzling her neck.

"I can't believe the change that has come over you—and so fast. You're like a completely different person. What have you done with the stern and always correct Dr. Jordan Walker?"

"He still exists, but you'll only see him in his clinic. When we're here alone, I'm Jordy, a little boy who once stood at the window outside the candy shop and has now been invited in."

"Oh, my God, were you really called Jordy?"

"Only once, when I was twelve, and I promised my sister Jessica that she would die a most painful death if she ever called me that again."

But he knew, if anyone could get away with calling him that now, it would be Kat.

FIFTEEN

When Kat awoke the next morning, she wondered if she had dreamed the evening before. Jordan had instantly become a different person. Once he decided to trust her with his vulnerability, he jumped in with both feet. She didn't believe he could be so impetuous, but perhaps he wasn't. He had admitted a long-standing interest.

After dinner, they spent the evening talking. Jordan confessed he had hesitated making a move on her because he didn't want Kat to feel she had to reciprocate in order to keep her job, or because they were sharing the apartment.

Kat laughed to herself as she remembered that she had told him in no uncertain terms that she wouldn't enter into a relationship with him or anyone else just to keep a roof over her head.

There was a gentle tap on her door that ended her reminiscing. "Kat, are you awake?"

"I'm awake, what's up?"

"Matt radioed the clinic," Jordan said, poking his head into her room. "One of his horses is showing symptoms of equine influenza. He wants me to come up to the ranch today if I'm able to get there."

"Are you going?"

"Of course. Even if he weren't my brother-in-law, I'd go. If he's right and the horse has influenza, it could spread through his stable. Do you feel up to an adventure?"

"Lead on, Macduff. I will follow you anywhere." Kat was grinning. She enjoyed teasing Jordan.

"Well, then, get up and get dressed. I'll fix breakfast this morning so we can eat sooner and be on our way."

"Aren't you going to tell me to dress warm?"

"No, I think you know the routine by now." Jordan winked.

Kat flew through her shower, and dressed again in the cold-weather gear she had worn the previous Friday. She was glad she'd washed clothes Friday evening after her parents had gone to their B&B. If this sort of thing was likely to happen throughout the fall and winter, she should probably buy more cold-weather gear.

Jordan was setting her breakfast on the table: coffee, hot steel-cut oatmeal, her own homemade whole-wheat toast, and natural peanut butter. "Slather your toast with peanut butter. You need protein and fat in this cold weather."

"Yes, doctor," Kat quipped, laughing at his protective behavior. Jordan was as bad as her brother Tony.

Jordan sat down across from her and started shoveling oatmeal into his mouth. One thing that could be said for him, Kat thought—he practiced what he preached.

The two of them made quick work of the after-breakfast chores and descended to the clinic. When Jordan told Torrey they were going, he asked her to radio Matt and tell him they were on their way, and if they weren't there in two hours, to send out the rescue teams.

Jordan checked the SUV to be certain he had packed all the supplies they might need, including emergency gear and an extra five gallons of gas. He picked Kat up and deposited her in the passenger seat. She didn't even protest this time. He put the truck into four-wheel drive and started off slowly. Even in four-wheel drive with steel-studded snow tires, the ice that formed overnight was challenging.

"Were you serious about taking two hours to get to the ranch?" Kat asked when they were finally on the road.

"I am. We'll be traveling far slower than we did on Friday, and we may encounter problems. From Spruce Creek north, the only road clearing is done by the locals. The state doesn't plow Guanella Pass Road during the winter."

"It's not winter yet," she teased. "It's still fall."

"Maybe on the calendar, but not in the high country. Winter's here, my love, and we'll be digging out until May."

Kat hugged herself when he called her *my love*. Did he even realize what he'd said? She thought not.

The road appeared undisturbed. She knew Matt had made his way up on Sunday afternoon, but snow had blown over his tracks and they no longer existed. Kat felt anxious, as if Jordan and she were the only two people in the world. She was glad that Jordan had asked for a rescue team if they weren't there in two hours. Kat thought he had been kidding, now she realized that he hadn't been.

Jordan broke her reverie when he asked, "What are you thinking?"

"The world is so still and we're the only two people on the planet. Where there are fields, the snow is pristine. In some places the limbs on the spruce trees bend low—in others the limbs are just dusted. The sky is as blue as I have ever seen it. Currier and Ives couldn't do this scenery justice."

"Are you studying to be a poet, Kat?"

"Stop being such a pragmatist. How many people ever get to see nature's glory like this?"

"I'm teasing you, Kat. You're right, the frozen landscape is beautiful, but so is a forest fire. Both are deadly. Don't ever forget that."

The SUV crept deliberately up the road. Jordan was a good driver, even in these nasty conditions. He didn't get impatient. He kept a steady speed, only turned the wheel when necessary and then very slowly. Since there was no traffic, he didn't need to worry about other vehicles.

When they finally reached the turnoff, it was identifiable because the ranch road had been roughly plowed to the highway.

"This is where the going gets rough," Jordan

warned Kat. "With the overhanging trees we're going to encounter ice and we'll not be able to see it in advance. So tighten your seatbelt and hang on."

Jordan dropped the transmission into low gear and turned onto the access road. Now they were traveling no faster than five miles an hour. Kat watched him struggle to keep the truck centered on the narrow lane. Hidden ruts and pot holes challenged him, pulling the wheel of the SUV this way and that. Jordan was doing physical battle, and she could see the strain on his face. She figured the best way she could help was to sit very still and not chatter at him.

Finally, after what seemed like forever, the ordeal was over and Jordan pulled into the level area in front of Matt's ranch house.

Matt hurried out to greet them. "Tough drive, bro?"

"You better believe it," Jordan replied, sighing.

Kat sat quietly in the passenger seat while Jordan climbed out of the truck. She didn't even protest when Jordan came to her side of the vehicle and lifted her out.

Matt gave them a knowing grin.

JORDAN WAS GREATLY RELIEVED THAT the first part of the ordeal was over. But he still had to drive back down the mountain. That was for later—for now, he wanted to focus on being a vet.

Matt led them inside the house. "Sit a spell and let the tension seep out. How about some coffee? I don't have any pastry to offer since Consuela is in California."

"We had breakfast before we left the clinic," Kat answered, "so we don't need pastries, but coffee would be a gift from the gods."

Jordan was grateful that she'd save him the effort of replying.

"Coming right up," Matt replied.

"Have you ever noticed how people here in the mountains are always offering food and hospitality?" Jordan said to Kat as Matt walked into the kitchen. "That doesn't happen when you're in the big city."

"I have a theory about that," Kat said as Matt returned with their coffee.

"A theory about what?" Matt asked as he handed Kat her cup of hot liquid.

"Jordan and I were just talking about how food and hospitality are the first things offered when entering a home here in the wilderness."

"This isn't wilderness, Kat," Jordan interjected.

"Almost," Kat replied. "But back to my theory. In the big city there are a multitude of public and private agencies to call on when you run up against something you can't do for yourself. Here, we can't exactly call road service if we slide off into a ditch."

"What does that have to do with food and hospitality?" Matt asked.

"By offering hospitality, we're assuring people that they can seek food, shelter and any other needed assistance from us," Kat continued. "For example, if we hadn't arrived here in two hours, you wouldn't radio the sheriff in Fairplay to come look for us. You would alert Jeremy to begin searching from his end and you would start out from here until one or the other of you had found us or met in the middle. Right?"

"I agree." Matt nodded. "The fact that you and Jordan would venture up here in these miserable driving conditions because I have a sick horse confirms your theory."

"For God's sake, Matt, don't make me sound as if I've done something heroic," Jordan said. "I'm a vet. This is my job."

Kat grinned at Matt. "I think you've

embarrassed him."

Jordan was relieved when Matt broke the tension. "Well, if this is your job, let's go look at my sick horse."

They drove in Jordan's SUV up the hill to the barn. Dodger, the horse in question, was in a stall at the far end. He was Matt's favorite saddle horse, a big gelded roan, strong and steady. Matt was keeping him as far away from the other animals as possible to prevent the spread of any infection.

Jordan asked Kat to bring him his black bag. The two of them gloved. Matt didn't bother— Dodger was his horse and he'd already handled him.

Jordan entered Dodger's stall carefully. While the animal wasn't known for kicking or biting, Jordan was taking no chances since the animal was sick.

Dodger stood placidly in his stall, laboring to breathe in and wheezing with every exhale. Jordan first did an external examination. He noted that Dodger had a nasal discharge. Next, Jordan used a long-line stethoscope to listen to the animal's heartbeat and gut sounds.

He turned to Kat with a grin on his face. "Have you ever taken a horse's temperature?"

"No, but if I had to guess, I'd wager I will be taking Dodger's temperature today."

"Right you are. But I'll walk you through the procedure."

Kat grimaced.

"Matt, please hobble Dodger's back legs," Jordan instructed.

"Will do," Matt replied.

"Kat, I'll hold his head so he can't turn and bite you. While I'm doing that, you take the thermometer—the big one with the lanyard attached—grease the thermometer well with petroleum jelly, slip the lanyard around Dodger's tail and secure it, then insert the thermometer rectally. Can you do that?"

"Piece of cake, but don't let go of his head."

They stood patiently until the digital thermometer beeped and Kat withdrew it. During the entire procedure, Dodger stood placidly, unconcerned about the abuse of his dignity.

"What's the reading?" Jordan asked.

"Ninety-nine," Kat replied. "Perfectly normal."

"His pulse and his respiration are just slightly elevated," Jordan told Matt. "I don't think he has equine flu, but I do think he is allergic to something here in the barn. Have you received new feed or hay recently?"

"I took delivery of some bales of straw just before the storm. Do you want to check?"

"Yup, let's check it out."

They went to the other side of the barn where the hay and straw were stored. Matt took a hook and broke open a bale of straw. Jordan rummaged around inside and pulled out a handful with minute amounts of mold.

"I think this is probably the problem," Jordan said. "The straw you're using for bedding has mold spores, probably baled while still damp. You've kept your hay dry and away from the straw so your feed doesn't appear to be contaminated. You need to get all the straw out of the barn and wash down the stalls."

"Going to be cold work," Matt grumbled, "but it'll get done."

"That's why you have hired hands," Jordan replied.

"So why is Dodger the only horse sick?" Matt asked changing the subject.

"He's obviously the most sensitive, but your other horses would be in similar shape before long if we hadn't caught this quickly."

"I'll contact my supplier, get him up here to pick up this stuff, and have him bring clean, dry straw."

"If the conditions were warmer, you could just put the horses out to pasture. But with all this snow on the ground, that's not a good idea," Jordan said. "I'll give Dodger a shot of antihistamine to start him on the road to recovery, and with the straw gone, he shouldn't have a relapse."

Jordan gathered the tools of his trade and replaced them in his medical bag. He put the used gloves in a sack to be disposed of later. Then he walked out of the barn with his arm around Kat. "You did good today. You didn't even flinch when I had you take Dodger's temperature."

"This wasn't the first time I've taken an animal's temperature. I just didn't have horse experience. Since Matt hobbled his back legs and you were hanging onto his head, I wasn't too concerned."

Jordan put his bag in the back of the SUV and then walked over to open the passenger door. With his arm still around Kat, he boosted her up onto the seat.

When they got into Matt's house, all three of them headed to the big sink in the laundry room. They dropped their coats while waiting for the water to warm. Then six arms were plunged under the running water, and they all scrubbed to the elbows. Even though Jordan and Kat had both been wearing gloves, they didn't want to risk cross contamination—plus the warm water felt good.

Kat was glad that Dodger's ailment, while serious, was easily fixed. She listened while Matt apologized for calling them up to the ranch, when the illness was one he could have identified himself if he had given some thought to the problem.

Jordan assured him that calling the vet when a horse was as sick as Dodger had been was always the right thing to do.

"Face it, Matt, you wouldn't have had an antihistamine on hand to administer. My visit was warranted."

Matt abruptly changed the subject. "Forgive me, Kat, if I embarrass you, but appearances lead me to believe something has changed between you two. How about it, Jordan—are you getting over your misogyny? Should I be listening for the sound of wedding bells?"

Kat felt the heat rise in her face and cast her eyes down, unable to look either man in the eye.

"Don't jump the gun, Matt. Nobody is talking about marriage here. Kat and I have just agreed to date," Jordan responded.

Date—is that what we've agreed to do? Jordan had suggested they become something more than friends—but exactly what, she'd not defined in her own mind. She appreciated Jordan's effort to keep the lid on their relationship. She knew it was only a matter of time before the level of their involvement—assuming that level escalated— became common knowledge to their friends and colleagues.

"Kat, I must applaud you. No one has succeeded in getting Jordan into a dating relationship. I don't suppose you would tell me your secret?"

"She has no secret, Matt," Jordan responded. "She just is what she is. She's honest, loyal, outspoken, and hardworking. I haven't run into another woman with those attributes since Torrey came into our lives when I was a child. So, of course I'm attracted," he said as he pulled her into a loose embrace.

"Jordan, stop. You're embarrassing me," Kat pleaded.

Jordan squeezed her closer and smiled.

"That's something else that has changed," Matt said. "Jordan is going around with a smile on his face. I'm surprised he can even get his facial muscles to respond since he's had no prior practice."

"Come on, Kat, we had best head back to the clinic. I'm tired of my brother-in-law picking on me."

Matt waited at the door for them. "All joking aside, I *am* happy that the two of you are discovering something between you. I hope your relationship develops into whatever you guys decide you want."

Jordan and Matt did the man-hug thing, and then Matt kissed Kat on her check. They said their goodbyes and, once again, started down the ranch road toward home.

The sun was higher in the sky and there were patches where ice had turned to mud. The descent was no easier than coming up had been earlier. Kat watched Jordan grip the wheel and she felt him tap the brake from time to time. Even though the truck was in first gear and four-wheel drive, the grade was steep enough in places to require the extra braking. They did some slipping and sliding, but Jordan never over-corrected or showed any sign of concern.

When they finally exited onto Guanella Pass Road, they both breathed a sigh of relief. The sun was bright overhead and almost blinding after the shade of the ranch road. They both reached for sunglasses. Their tracks from earlier in the morning were the only sign of travel on the scenic byway.

Jordan was more relaxed, so Kat felt she could talk without distracting him. "How do you feel about Matt's conclusions concerning us?"

"I'm not surprised. I know Torrey will tumble the first time she sees us together. Matt is just as observant as she is. You've made a significant change in my life."

"You *do* seem more relaxed, but what other changes have I made?"

"I'm happier than I've ever been. Getting up in the morning, I look forward to each day. I'm enjoying my work. And when you're with me, my life is sweet. Everyone who knows me will see the change, and those who know you will understand why. The best day of my life was when you came storming into my office and berated me for not having a senior discount program."

"I still blush when I think of that."

"You shouldn't. On that day I witnessed your honesty, your loyalty, and your outspokenness. I took a little longer to observe how hard you work."

Kat frowned and stayed quiet for a minute.

"What's wrong?" Jordan asked.

"I'm happy that I have all those attributes, but

do you find me attractive? I find *you* attractive."

Jordan stopped the SUV in the middle of the road, set the brake, and reached across the bench seat. Releasing her seat belt, he pulled Kat into his arms.

"What are you doing?" Kat squealed. "We're stopped in the middle of the highway."

"I find you so deliciously attractive that I must use all my self-control to keep my hands off you," Jordan breathed as he nuzzled her ear. "And I don't think we need to be concerned about traffic on the highway. Come here, wench, and let me show you how attractive you are."

Jordan pulled her along the seat until she was in his lap. She could definitely feel how attractive he found her.

"Now do you have any doubts?"

"Umm . . . no." She wrapped her arms around his shoulders and squirmed closer. Snuggling wasn't easy to do with them both bundled up, but she did her best. She leaned forward and kissed him.

"Kat, if you don't stop right now, I won't be responsible for my actions. I would rather our first intimate experience not be in the front seat of a cold SUV."

Kat wiggled once more, and then scooted

back into the passenger seat. "You're right, of course. But then, you're always right, aren't you?"

She was starting to think it was just part of his charm.

SIXTEEN

A s they pulled into Spruce Creek, Jordan remembered he'd never asked Torrey about a prior employee with an affinity for cloves. He made a mental note to do so first thing when they got into the clinic.

He turned to Kat. "Can you believe it was just last week that we were in Denver?" he asked. "So much has happened since then. We had lunch in Golden; we went to Matt's ranch and inoculated goats; we hosted your family for a weekend; we survived a blizzard; we've become a couple; and we've been back up to the ranch again."

"We have had a busy six days," Kat responded. "Is there a point to the reiteration of our hectic existence?"

"Yes, I haven't yet spoken to Torrey about cloves." Mentally, Jordan blamed his forgetfulness on the many *things* that had been happening—but he accepted he was at fault.

"I'd forgotten the entire discussion," Kat said, shaking her head. "It seems as if it took place a long time ago. But if Torrey can remember someone who smelled of cloves, we should learn who and share the information with Turner so he can solve the crime, and I can move into my own space again."

Jordan blanched. "Kat, you're not serious. You don't plan to move out if the culprit is found, do you?"

"Not if you don't want me to."

"Well, that's settled then. I don't want you to. The only move I want you to make is into my bedroom."

He watched her face redden. With her pale skin and freckles, her reactions were an open book. He had embarrassed her by being so explicit. He needed to avoid doing so when others were around. They would understand her reactions as easily as he did. He wasn't quite ready to have their intimate relationship go public.

Jordan pulled the SUV into the garage behind the clinic, and lifted Kat to the ground. It had become the natural thing to do. The two of them disposed of the waste and restocked the vehicle making certain everything they would need was in the truck if they were called out unexpectedly. Then they took their cold-weather gear back up to the apartment.

Since they would probably not be alone again during the entire afternoon, Jordan pulled Kat into an embrace and kissed her deeply. "We'll take up tonight where we left off in the truck."

When they entered the clinic, their professional demeanor was back in place. If they were slightly red faced, it could be attributed to the outdoor temperatures.

Jordan approached his office manager. "Torrey, please radio Matt and let him know we're safely back. Then grab today's schedule and come into my office."

Torrey lifted an eyebrow, but did as requested. Meanwhile, Kat started reviewing the files that were pulled for the afternoon's appointments. Jordan knew she would go about her job as if nothing had changed.

When Torrey came into Jordan's office, he asked her to close the door and be seated.

"What's up?" she inquired.

"Torrey, do you remember a prior employee

who smoked clove cigarettes? He always smelled of cloves."

"Vaguely," she said with a nod. "He wasn't here long. His name was Rob. No, Ron. Or Ray." She tapped her cheek thoughtfully. "Wait, no—I've got it. His name was Roger, and he went by Rog most of the time. You fired him because you found him kicking a dog."

"I'd forgotten all about that. It was a while ago. Bring me his file, and nose around among the staff to see if anyone is in touch with him or knows where he might be right now. And Torrey—don't mention cloves."

"You think he might be the burglar who attacked Kat?"

"It's possible. Thanks, Torrey, that's all." Jordan turned to his phone, preparing to call Turner and tell him what they had turned up.

"Not quite." Torrey stayed planted in the chair. "Something's happening between you and Kat. You're looking mighty smug."

"Damn, do you have our apartment bugged? I thought it might take you at least an hour to tumble."

"Jordan, I raised you from the time you were six years old. I work with you every day. I know you better than either Jess or Jeremy. You're a changed person. Now tell me why."

"Kat and I have agreed to date."

"Agreed to date? Good heavens, Jordan, you sound like a nineteenth century snob who's been formally granted courting privileges by the girl's father."

"Almost. You know her family spent the weekend with us. Her father wanted to know my intentions. That prompted me to admit I want to know her outside of work."

"Good heavens, boy. She's been living in your apartment for months. Are you telling me that you don't know anything about her except on a professional level? What do you two talk about when you're up there alone?"

Jordan slid down in his chair a little before answering. "Food—books—animals. I've learned a few things about her life, but not a lot."

"And, of course, you haven't shared anything about yours."

"No, not really. I'm not comfortable scraping at that scab."

Jordan watched as Torrey ran her hands through her hair. He could tell she wanted to get up and pace, but his office was too small.

"Torrey, give it a rest. I am what I am. Kat may be able to change that, but only time will tell." He smiled. "I do know that right now, I'm happier and more content than I've ever been. She may be the one woman, besides you, that I can trust."

Torrey stood to leave. "Okay, Jordan, I'll back off. But I'll be watching."

"And Torrey . . ." She looked his way. "Don't pester Kat. Give her breathing room."

"I'll bring that file you want," Torrey said, smiling knowingly as she walked through the door.

CURLED IN THE OVERSTUFFED CHAIR in front of the fire, Kat once again was thinking about what she wanted to do in the apartment. Now that they were a *couple* she wanted to talk to Jordan before she made any changes. She didn't want to presume and possibly drive a wedge into their tentative relationship. No matter what he said, this was still Jordan's home.

But Kat already had decided they needed additional phones in the apartment, so she asked Torrey to have extensions put in the kitchen and Jordan's den. They could all ring on the same number. She was certain Jordan wouldn't object. As it was, when the phones were on night and weekend service, they rang in Jordan's bedroom. With additional handsets, Kat could answer after-hours calls.

When she heard him come in, she called out, "I'm in front of the fire."

"Of course you are," he said, walking into the room. "Where else would you be?"

He bent down, kissed her, then picked her up and settled into the chair with her in his lap.

"Oh, you're cold. I was warm before you came in," she said with a shiver.

He cuddled her closer. "We'll both be warm just as soon as you share your body heat."

Kat felt a contentment she'd not known before. "Jordan, would you mind if I made the apartment more homelike? With things such as scatter rugs, pictures—stuff like that."

"Kat, I've told you, this is your place, too. You can do anything you want to make us more comfortable. I certainly won't object."

"You're sure?"

"I'm sure. But right now I don't want to talk about redecorating. I want to make out with my girl. Kiss me like you mean it."

Kat leaned forward tentatively. She touched her lips to Jordan's, then put her hands in his hair and pulled into him. She felt his five-o'clock shadow scratch against her face—such an intimate feeling.

He did his part, letting his hands roam over her body, his tongue touching the seam of her lips. The petting session might have gone on all night except that Kat's stomach growled loudly.

She sat up abruptly, feeling the blush rise up beneath her skin. "I'm sorry, Jordan. That was rude of my stomach, but I'm hungry. Remember, we never got lunch today."

"Then I suppose I must feed you." He laughed as he set her on her feet.

They moved into the kitchen. Acting in tandem, they made quick work of fixing dinner. When they neared the end of their meal, Kat asked, "Jordan, could we get a cat?"

"Are you telling me you don't get enough of cats and dogs all day long?"

"Those are other people's pets. I want one of our own, a pet to cuddle in the chair when I settle down to read, an animal to greet me when I walk in the door, something to make me feel needed."

"What? You can't tell me I fail to make you feel needed."

"There's a difference. You want me, but you don't need me. You're not dependent upon me for your wellbeing. A pet would be dependent, almost like a child."

Jordan stood and walked to Kat's side of the table. He pulled her up into his arms. "You're wrong, Kat. I *am* dependent upon you for my wellbeing. Since my mother abandoned us, I have never felt loved and treasured. I need that like I need air and light and warmth. You give me those things with no strings attached. If I'm not dependent upon you, I cannot imagine who would be."

"Jordan, that is the most moving thing anyone has ever said to me."

The ringing of the phone broke the mood. When Jordan moved to the bedroom to answer it, Kat started brewing after-dinner coffee and cleared the table.

"Jeremy is coming by for dessert. He wants to talk about our break-in suspect."

"Why in the world did he call? He's never phoned before—he just shows up."

Jordan grinned sheepishly. "I think word has reached him of our altered circumstances. He didn't want to intrude if we were in the middle of something."

Kat wiped the table clean with forceful swipes before setting coffee cups and dessert plates out. She needed to vent her embarrassment.

"How can that be? Surely he hasn't been up to the ranch. Isn't Matt the only one who knows about us?"

"Torrey has figured us out. She confronted me when we were in my office this afternoon. I'm certain she's Jeremy's source."

"Do we have scarlet letters across our foreheads that we're so obvious to people like Matt and Torrey?"

"Kat, do you remember what I was like the day you confronted me about Mr. Gardner's cat? I was completely uninterested in his problems, or in the problems of any of the pet owners who came to me to treat their animals. I was aloof, a nonparticipating member of the community. I was concerned with only one thing, containing the mental pain that was my daily existence."

Kat nodded.

"Both Torrey and Matt know me well. They know the grief and guilt that ate at me. They tolerated a mean-spirited curmudgeon because I was family, but they didn't like that person. I'm no longer who I was. Both of them have seen the changes in me and know you are the cause."

Once again, they were interrupted when Jeremy tapped at the door. There was a pause before he came walking in.

Kat welcomed him. "You don't need to knock, Jeremy. You can still come in without waiting for an invitation."

"Just wanted to give you guys time to break from the clutch." He stepped forward and hugged Jordan. "Welcome to the human race, bro."

Jeremy turned and hugged Kat. "Thanks for rescuing Jordan," he said, kissing her on the cheek.

She blushed, and then turned to serve dessert and pour coffee. "Tell us what you've learned about the suspect."

Jeremy didn't discuss the source of his information—only that after Torrey told him what Jordan suspected, that he'd snooped a bit. He believed that Roger was now living in Fairplay. He promised to share his information with Turner. Finishing his coffee, he stood to leave.

"Jeremy," Kat said, "you don't need to rush off. You just got here."

"I think Jordan would disagree with you. The sooner I'm gone, the happier he'll be." He turned to his brother with his mischievous grin. "Right, bro?"

Jordan nodded, thanked his brother for the

information he'd uncovered about Roger, and then unceremoniously nudged Jeremy out and locked the door behind him.

"No more interruptions," Jordan emphasized. "No matter how dire the emergency, we will not be disturbed again this evening." He pulled Kat into his arms. "Is tonight too soon? Are you ready to share my bed?"

Kat tensed in his embrace.

"Relax, sweetheart, we don't have to do anything unless you want to," he assured her.

She knew bright red color rose to her hairline. Kat could never hide her embarrassment; her face was like a neon billboard.

"I'm afraid, Jordan. I have no experience, and I don't want you to be disappointed."

Looking at her with awe, Jordan held his hands on her shoulders and stepped back a few inches. "Kat, are you telling me you're a virgin?"

"Yes, but I'm not ashamed of it." She lifted her chin defiantly. "Before you, there wasn't anyone I wanted to be intimate with. I'm not certain I'm ready yet. Can we just snuggle for a while?"

"We can snuggle for as long as you want. How do you want to go about snuggling?"

"Can I sleep in your bed—get comfortable

being next to you?"

"If that's what you want, Kat, I will do my best to control my baser instincts." He wiggled his eyebrows in an exaggerated leer.

"Oh, am I asking too much? Will I be making you miserable?"

"Kat, I was teasing," Jordan said, smiling. "I will not be overcome in the night and attack your body. I can be content and comfortable lying beside you. We will not do anything else unless you choose to."

Just like that, the tension disappeared from her body. Kat rushed through her nightly preparations, and then braided her hair loosely into a single plait. In her own bedroom, she put on a flannel granny gown.

She slipped across the hall and into Jordan's room. The lamp was dimmed and the bedding had been turned back. Jordan's bed was higher off the floor than the one in her room, so she had to scramble to climb in. By the time Jordan quietly entered the room she had relaxed and, curled on her side, was lightly dozing.

Kat was aware of his presence, but her relaxed state was so comfortable she didn't want to rouse. Sleepily, she watched him remove his clothes. Suddenly she tensed, remembering that he slept only in his briefs. But surely in winter he wore more than that to bed. But no, he didn't. He climbed in next to her, dressed—or undressed— just as he had been the night that Jeremy arrived.

God, he was gorgeous. He was barrel-chested and long limbed—built solid like an athlete—but his build was the result of hard work, not time spent in a gym. Chocolate-colored hair scattered across his chest, arrowed down his stomach and disappeared into his briefs. Her fingers itched to tangle themselves in that chest hair.

Jordan lay flat on his back. His hand crept out to touch her fingers. "Kat, are you awake?"

She thought of not answering, but decided that would be dishonest. "I'm awake, but just barely."

"Good night, sweetheart. You and I will talk in the morning." He turned onto his side, away from her.

"Good night, Jordan," she said to his back.

When she woke in the morning, warm and rested, Kat realized she was spooned against Jordan's back. Her head rested between his shoulder blades and her arm was draped over his middle. His very sexy butt was nestled against her pelvis.

She stiffened, and her first instinct was to pull

away. Their position was certainly intimate. Then she realized that, since she was draped around Jordan, it was her body that had sought his. He was an innocent party.

"Good morning, Kat," he said in a gravelly morning voice.

"How did you know I'm awake?" she asked.

"You tensed when you discovered our embrace. Don't worry; I know you weren't trying to have your way with me. You just got cold during the night and sought a warm body."

Embarrassed, she rolled away from him. Instantly she felt colder. "You don't mind?"

"Mind, why would I mind? Sleeping in your embrace provided me with the best night's sleep I've had in ages." He rolled out of the bed. "But now I need to answer a call of nature."

Kat followed him out of the bedroom. While he headed for the bathroom, she went into her room for her robe and slippers. She hadn't thought to bring them into Jordan's room before going to bed.

Her next stop was the living room to stir up the fire, then the kitchen to start the coffee. She could hear the water running when she returned to her own room to lay out her clothes for the day. Jordan was in the shower.

When he came out of the bathroom with only a towel around his waist, she admired his beautiful body. She had seen him like this only once before, months ago when he rushed into her room to save her from Jeremy.

Now she was reminded of how he had appeared the night before when he came to bed. His shoulders and arms were well developed. He had to be strong to wrestle and lift some of the animals he treated. He had a washboard stomach; there wasn't an inch of fat on his torso. And his thighs spurred her imagination. At that moment, she would have gladly allowed him to take her virginity.

But work would not be denied. She entered the shower and started her own preparations for a day in the clinic.

When they met in the kitchen she was unsure how to talk with him. But Jordan had no such hesitation. He hugged her and said, "So, how is my best girl? Did you rest well last night?"

"I did," she said. "Your bed is more comfortable than mine."

"Well, then," he said, "you had best sleep in my bed again tonight."

"Okay, I'll do that."

SEVENTEEN

Remembering she'd failed to eat lunch the day before, Kat made a point of going up to the apartment to fix a sandwich and drink a glass of milk. She was rinsing her dishes when she heard Jordan coming up the stairs. Even though they worked in the same clinic, much of the day passed without them meeting or talking. So she was delighted that the two of them might have a few minutes together.

Jordan came through the door with a mewing fuzzy creature in his arms. He placed the fluff ball in Kat's hands. "You wanted a kitten—I give you a kitten."

"Oh, Jordan, this little one is precious. Where did you get—her?" she asked turning the black and white baby over to determine the gender.

"Mrs. Engle brought Kirby's kittens in for their second shots. She asked if she could put a notice on the bulletin board saying she had kittens to give to good homes. So I took the cutest kitten off her hands and now she is in your hands. What will you name her?"

"Don't know yet. I need to get to know her so her name will be appropriate to her personality. Thank you, you're a love."

Kat, holding the kitten in one hand, wrapped her other arm around Jordan's torso and pulled him in for a kiss. She intended to give him just a peck, a sign of gratitude, but heat flared and the kiss turned into more. Then the kitten protested and the embrace ended sooner than either of them wanted.

"Take her back down to the clinic and put her in a boarding cage," Jordan said. "She shouldn't be alone up here until we have all the necessary kitten furnishing. And put her on the schedule to be spayed. She's just twelve weeks now."

"Yes, doctor," Kat said in her most professional voice. Jordan just grinned at her as she left to return to work.

After getting the kitten safely settled in a cage near other animals so that she wouldn't be lonely, Kat went in search of Torrey.

"I need kitten food, a litter box, food and water dishes, and anything else you think we will need for a new baby," she gushed excitedly when she found the office manager. "Jordan and I are adopting one of Kirby's recent litter, and I'm so excited I can't think."

Torrey grinned back at her. "Well, you just march yourself out to reception and get one of the pamphlets that we give to new cat owners. The pamphlet will provide a list of the *must haves* and the *might wants*. We don't keep things like pet beds and scratching posts on hand. You'll need to purchase those."

"Oh, I can't imagine why I didn't think of that."

"Because you are not thinking—you're in love."

"In love?" Kat asked, shocked.

"With your new pet, of course." With a wink, Torrey turned and walked away.

At the end of the work day, Kat gathered together the items Torrey had set aside for the new kitten. She made one trip to the apartment with the accumulation and then returned to bring the baby home.

When the kitten was set loose on her own, she set about investigating her new digs. She was inquisitive and not the least bit timid. Within the first thirty minutes, she managed to get into a wastebasket, knock books off the lowest shelf of the bookcase, and fall into her drinking water. After Kat cleaned up the spilt water and dried the kitten off, the little thing sat down on a pillow and promptly fell asleep by the fire.

"I know what I'm going to name you, missy. Your name is going to be Calamity Jane. You are a disaster looking for a place to happen."

Kat set up Calamity Jane's litter box in the laundry room. She made her a temporary bed of old towels near the fireplace, and set dry food and fresh water for her in the kitchen. When she was done, Kat collapsed into her favorite chair in front of the fire. She decided that taking care of one little kitten on the loose was more work than taking care of a clinic full of animals.

When the kitten awoke, she wandered around the apartment crying. When Kat picked her up and put her in her lap, the crying stopped. But as soon as she was put down, her plaintive mewing started up again.

When Jordan came in, Kat told him she was concerned the kitten was sick because she wouldn't stop crying unless Kat held her.

"She misses her litter mates. She'll settle

down. But you shouldn't hold her too much or you'll become her slave. Have you decided on a name yet?"

Kat told him she was going to call her Calamity Jane, and she told him why.

When he stopped laughing, he asked Kat where she had set the litter box.

"In the laundry room. Is that okay?"

He nodded. "Good place. You should put Jane's food, water, and bed in there, as well. If she's as bad as you say she is, we can't have her wandering free during the night."

"But, Jordan, she'll be cold and lonely."

"Kat, you're overly emotional. Calamity Jane is a cat, she has a fur coat—and the laundry room is warm enough. She'll be fine."

"Okay. I know you're right."

After dinner, Jordan took an old pillow from the linen closet and the towels that Kat had used to make Jane's bed. He put a piece of plastic on the laundry room's tile floor, wrapped the pillow in the towels Kat had provided, and made a cozy bed for Calamity Jane. He put a loudly ticking clock in the room as well, to provide company for Jane. When Kat and Jordan went to bed, they could hear the kitten crying.

Kat, in sympathy, wanted to cry, too.

EIGHTEEN

More than a week had passed since Calamity Jane joined the household. Kat and Jordan had purchased a puffy cat bed— Jordan had not been amused when Kat suggested purchasing a gaudy piece of furniture that looked like a lounge for Queen Cleopatra.

Other necessary purchases included a skyscraper cat tree, a covered litter box to preserve Jane's privacy, and a gravity dry-food feeder. Calamity Jane also acquired a roommate. Because Jane was so lonely when Jordan and Kat were at work, Kat had prevailed on Jordan to adopt another of Kirby's offspring. Mrs. Engle was delighted to give yet another kitten to a good home.

Brando, the new addition, was as lazy as his

sister was energetic. He was content to eat and sleep. Jane pestered him unmercifully, trying to get him to join her in making trouble. If she successfully engaged his interest, he would follow her lethargically, but he wasn't into adventure. Eventually, though, the two of them would be found curled around each other in the puffy cat bed. Since their coats were so similar, difficulty lay in trying to determine where one cat left off and the other began.

The kids, as Kat called them, underwent the surgeries necessary to keep them from breeding. They were allowed to recover overnight in the clinic before returning to the apartment. Even Jane was sedate for a day or two before returning to her effervescent self.

Kat, assuming that Jordan would be hosting Thanksgiving for his brother and brother-in-law, put her efforts to making the changes in the apartment to accomplish what she had envisioned. She spent the afternoon online searching for items to make their living quarters cozy and warm.

All the rooms in the apartment were painted in neutral colors. Since she had no intention of repainting, nor did she think that Jordan would be willing to do so, she decided to add color with curtains, drapes, and rugs. She loved that she was making a home for Jordan. For the kitchen where he spent so much of his time, she found bright red and yellow café curtains with matching valance and long ruffled swags. The curtains were decorated with red roosters and yellow chicks, not too feminine, she decided. She added red place mats to the order. And then, impulsively, she also ordered a matching three-piece stove set including a towel, mitt, and pot holder. Finally, she decided to replace the everyday dishes with red flowered stoneware. Her intention was that mornings would be bright and cheerful, even in the dead of winter. She would start Jordan's day right.

From kitchen merchandise she moved her purchasing efforts into their shared bedroom. Jordan would want the room to reflect his masculinity. No ruffled curtains in this room— nothing too formal or too cutesy. She found deep blue thermal drapes with flecks of silver that seemed perfect. Warm and intimate was the ambience she was looking for. There were matching pillow shams and a duvet cover, so Kat ordered those, as well.

What she really wanted for Jordan's bedroom were braided rag rugs to put next to the bed so that the first thing her feet touched in the morning was not the cold floor. When she started looking, her breath was taken away by how expensive rugs were. But she kept searching and found jute at prices she felt she could afford. Actually, she preferred the oval rugs woven with a checkerboard of muted colors over the far more costly offerings she had seen. She ordered four, two for Jordan's room and two for the guest room.

Deciding she had spent enough money for one day, she ordered window hardware from a single source for both the kitchen and the bedroom. Now all she had to do was wait.

She had spent much of the morning online and she realized, as she closed down her laptop, that the kittens had not been around to bother her, which was unusual. She hoped that she would simply find them curled up together pursuing Brando's favorite pastime, but she suspected that would be too good to be true.

When she went in search of the cats, she found the bathroom door ajar. The wastebasket had been upended and debris scattered around the bathroom. Additionally, there were claw marks in the toilet paper and at least half the paper had been unrolled all over the bathroom floor. Brando was curled up asleep in the middle of the mess. After what was certainly Jane's work, the naughty kitten had abandoned her brother to take the blame while she scouted new avenues of trouble.

Kat chuckled to herself as she moved Brando to a more comfortable bed in the living room. Then she began the task of cleaning up the mess. Fortunately, there was no real damage done, just mischief. Kat was beginning to think that 'Mischief' would have been as appropriate a name as Calamity Jane. While Kat was searching for the naughty little girl, Jordan came into the apartment and called out, "Kat, I'm home."

"Of course you are," she said as she came and wrapped her arms around him. "Is everything okay in the clinic?"

"The temperature is a bit chilly down there, so I turned up the heat. I'll check on the animals before we go to bed and make certain they're warm enough for the night."

"We can always throw some additional bedding into the kennels if the temperature drops too far," Kat suggested. "Just like we did during the blizzard. And put the dogs together."

"We have one animal who is a vicious fighter. He won't be going into the kennel with any of the others. And I don't want you trying to feed or water him. He's big enough to overwhelm you."

"Will he need to be put down?"

"If his owner fails to come and claim him."

"That's so heartbreaking," Kat said sadly. "Dogs aren't naturally vicious; they have to be trained to be mean."

"I know, but this dog is what he is. We shouldn't worry about the strays. Tell me what you've been doing all morning."

Kat laughed. "Are you sure you want to know?"

"Why not?"

"Because I've been spending money. I bought curtains for the kitchen and drapes for the bedroom."

"How much money can you spend on curtains and drapes?" Jordan asked.

"True, the curtains and drapes weren't too expensive. But then I bought other stuff to go with the window coverings."

"What stuff, Kat? Have you put me in the poor house?" Jordan was grinning, so Kat knew he was teasing.

"Place mats and dishes for the kitchen, rugs and bedding for your room. But I'm paying for everything. I wasn't spending your money."

"If you decide to move out, are you taking these items with you?"

"I'm not moving out unless you tell me to, and then I would try to change your mind. But if I were, I wouldn't take the stuff with me. They were bought to be used here."

"I'm not going to tell you to move out. I need you to warm my bed on these cold winter nights. But since you wouldn't take the purchases with you, then I'll pay for them—no matter how much money you spent."

Jordan pulled Kat into his embrace. She was well aware that, when Jordan wanted to stop a discussion and have his point of view prevail, he always encircled her with his arms and pulled her close for a kiss. She knew he was doing that now, but she would let him succeed—this time.

NINETEEN

Kat had become more comfortable sleeping with Jordan. Climbing into his bed each night and awakening in his arms each morning seemed perfectly natural. But she understood if the relationship was going to move forward to true intimacy, she must give Jordan permission. She was in the driver's seat.

Early one morning Kat decided that, while she was nervous, she was now anxious to take the next step. When she'd awakened, she'd felt Jordan hard against her hip, his arm slung over her stomach as he spooned around her. His closeness gave her a tingle low in her belly. She wanted more than just his embrace.

She took his hand and moved his fingers up to cover her breast. At first, nothing happened.

Then they tightened, gently squeezing. He nibbled at her ear and whispered, "Does this mean what I think?"

"What do you think?" Kat asked.

"I think that you are ready," he said pulling her closer. "I'll be very gentle. You can stop me at any time if you become frightened."

"I trust you, Jordan. Show me now how to feel like a woman—how to please you."

So, on the Sunday before Thanksgiving, Kathleen Bridget Morelli lost her virginity and learned what all the romance authors wrote about.

Noon came before Jordan and Kat ventured into the kitchen in search of coffee and sustenance. When they let the cats out of the laundry room, they were treated to a vocal scolding from Calamity Jane about the injustice of being confined.

"I think," Jordan said, "that we can give the kittens free run of the apartment. They know where their litter box is and its purpose. We can move their food to the kitchen; the cat tree and their bed can take up residence in the living room. What do you think?"

"Can we trust their behavior?" Kat asked.

"How much trouble can two little kittens get

into?" Jordan said with a shrug.

Eventually, Kat and Jordan would learn the answer to that question.

Jeremy showed up that afternoon while they were watching the Denver Broncos on TV. The Broncos were playing the Oakland Raiders, their archrival, and the game was a contentious one. So when Jeremy arrived, there was no discussion about anything except football.

When Denver finally defeated Oakland in overtime, Jordan turned off the TV. "Okay, Jeremy, I suspect you didn't come just to watch football. What's on your mind?"

"Thanksgiving is next Thursday, and I'm wondering if I'm going to receive an invitation to dinner?"

"Have I ever failed to invite you?"

"Of course not, but things are different now. Kat's living with you, and she's more than just a roommate. So, I expect she has something to say about holiday dinner arrangements."

Kat blushed but spoke up in spite of her mild embarrassment. "I have no intention of changing anything between you and your brother. If Jordan chooses, Thanksgiving will be as always for you two. I just hope I'm invited to dinner."

"Okay, folks, let me make this clear," Jordan

spoke up. "Thanksgiving dinner will be the same except there will now be a hostess present. Kat, that hostess will be you. I'll invite Torrey and Matt, just like every year. Jeremy, consider this your invitation. I just wish that Jessie could be here. Now, are there any questions?"

"Is the menu carved in stone, or may I make a contribution?" Kat asked.

"Of course you can contribute. But I warn you, each family member has something special that he or she brings, so you will need to provide something not already spoken for. Matt brings dessert because Consuela bakes pumpkin and pecan pies for him. Jeremy brings the wine. Torrey brings a cranberry relish that's as good as dessert. I do the turkey and dressing and the other side dishes."

"Would you mind if I prepared a green bean side dish? Not that disgusting recipe with the canned mushroom soup and onion rings. All the ingredients for my creation are fresh and can be organic if we can get organic green beans at this time of year here in the mountains."

"Not a problem—I'll be the purveyor of fresh organic produce. What else do you need?"

"Bacon, onion, and lemon, all of which we have on hand," Kat responded. "The recipe is very simple, but that's what makes it so good."

"Sounds as if your dish is an appropriate addition to our menu."

"Jordan, one other thing, do you think we could invite my family?"

"Of course we can. Do you really think they'll come?"

"Probably not, especially after what happened with the weather the last time they were here. But maybe Tony will."

"Then, by all means, you must invite your parents and your brother."

TWENTY

Jordan greeted a Thanksgiving Day that dawned cold and crisp. As expected, Bridget and Emilio Morelli had declined Jordan's invitation. They had plans elsewhere, but Tony was expected.

Kat baked homemade cinnamon rolls for breakfast. She'd set the dough to rise in the back of the oven before going to bed the night before. She admitted to Jordan they weren't especially healthy fare, but since she only made them for special occasions she didn't think they were a health hazard.

Agreeing with Kat's assessment, Jordan ate three rolls and four pieces of bacon before beginning his preparations for Thanksgiving dinner. The cats were underfoot in the kitchen, drawn by the lovely aromas of chicken broth and raw turkey. Jordan chased the cats out, and Kat ran the vacuum. Their once-a-week housekeeper had quit because she claimed an allergy to feline dander. Jordan suspected the housekeeper was more afraid of cats than she was allergic.

Kat had easily assumed the duties of changing and washing the linens, dusting and vacuuming. Jordan pitched in, as well, assuming responsibility for emptying litter boxes, cleaning toilets, and mopping floors, all of which he knew were Kat's least favorite things. Jordan experienced a twinge of unease when he admitted to himself that sharing the household chores made them even more of a couple.

He had just put the stuffed bird into the oven when Matt and Jeremy arrived. Tony followed on their heels only minutes later. Kat stuck her head into the kitchen to say hello and then backed out quickly. Four large men in the kitchen were three too many. The cats apparently agreed, because after following her to the kitchen, they too exited in a hurry. Jordan chased the men out with instructions to turn the TV to the Detroit Lions game and leave him alone so he could finish clean-up.

He had followed them into the living room,

when Jeremy wrapped his arms around Kat and planted a kiss on her forehead. "Happy Thanksgiving, little sister."

Matt kissed her cheek, tendering the same sentiments.

When Tony hugged her he held on, and then asked pointedly, "What do these two guys know that I don't?"

Jordan watched Kat look into Tony's eyes, aware that her brother might not be happy with her current situation. But before she could answer, Jordan spoke up. "Kat and I are now a couple. She makes me happy, and I try very hard to do the same for her."

"This change came about awfully sudden, didn't it?" Tony asked caustically. "What happened to what you told my father about being just roommates and there was no other relationship?"

"I also told your father the decision would be entirely up to Kat if things were to change," Jordan snapped back.

"Stop, Tony," Kat said sharply. "I am not a little girl for you to act the part of big brother protector. I'm old enough to make my own choices. I have freely chosen to enter into an intimate relationship with Jordan. Besides, I was just following Mother's instructions."

"Whoa," Jeremy sputtered, "too much information. You aren't leaving anything to my imagination."

Matt grinned but kept silent.

"Guys, I apologize for the public display of domestic fireworks. But Tony has always been able to push my buttons." Kat pulled away from her sibling, "Tony, please shake hands with Jordan. I don't want my brother and my lover at each other's throats."

By now, all four men were as red in the face as Kat. Tony did, however, reach out his hand to Jordan.

Matt spoke up. "We're all family here. And Jordan, you did say that two of the things you like most about Kat are that she is outspoken and honest."

"Is she ever," Jeremy mumbled.

Breaking the tension, Kat offered food. "How about I bring out beer and snacks for you to enjoy while watching football?" Without waiting for an answer, she darted into the kitchen.

"I should help her," Jordan said, following in her footsteps.

Out of sight of the guests, Jordan pulled Kat into his embrace. He could feel the *fight or flight* tension drain from her body. When she started to speak he shushed her. "Just let me hold you."

After a few moments, she pulled loose. "Those guys will come in here looking for food if I don't get out there with the promised snacks."

Jordan pulled cold beer from the refrigerator while Kat arranged crackers on a platter.

"Jordan, while you're in the fridge, can you get the relish tray I prepared?"

When they appeared in the living room Jeremy piped up, "What took you guys so long? Did you get distracted?"

Jordan stared hard at his sibling. "Jeremy, if you plan on eating Thanksgiving dinner with us, you better behave. You have stirred up enough trouble for one day."

"Me? What have I done?"

"You called me little sister and started the whole brouhaha," Kat said.

"But you are," he said with a shrug. "Or, at least, you will be soon, I expect."

"Jeremy, two things—one, you should have allowed me time to tell my brother about my relationship with Jordan, but you didn't. And two, since Jordan hasn't proposed nor have I, if and when I become your little sister remains to be seen."

"Well, if he doesn't ask you soon, he's a fool."

"Jeremy, butt out." Jordan sounded angry, and it appeared as if Jeremy finally realized he had gone too far.

"I'm sorry, Kat." Jeremy appeared sincere.

"Apology accepted," Kat responded. "Now, let's watch some football."

The tension in the room abated somewhat as cold beer was consumed along with cheese and crackers. The cats snuck back into the room and tried to beg cheese. When human attention was elsewhere, they even tried to help themselves. When that didn't work, Brando decided he was ready for a nap and crawled into Jeremy's lap. Jeremy further relaxed and started participating in the discussion of bad calls and good plays. Soon, everyone was involved in the traditional Thanksgiving pastime of being an armchair quarterback.

Torrey arrived toward the end of the Detroit game. Jordan watched as Kat escaped into the kitchen with her, both of them intent on avoiding male testosterone.

Leaving Brando to his favorite pastime—sleeping—Calamity Jane joined the women in the kitchen.

THANKSGIVING DINNER PASSED PEACEABLY enough after the fireworks surrounding Jeremy's greeting. The cats were banished to the laundry room so that their strident begging didn't cause distress. Jordan allowed them to lick the taste of turkey from his fingers before washing his hands and sitting down to dinner.

Tony offered a prayer before dinner, which seemed to mellow the raw edges of stressed personalities. As the prayer circled the table, each person shared the God-given gift for which each felt most grateful.

When they began eating, Torrey, apparently aware of some underlying tension, led the discussion away from the personal to the mundane. She started with small talk about the weather which led to other topics.

They talked about football and which teams were expected to make the Super Bowl. They were in agreement that, after the Thanksgiving Day game, the Detroit Lions were an unlikely choice. They moaned about the Denver Broncos and repeated the slogan most often uttered by Denver fans—*wait until next year.*

They talked about high-country ranching, the problems inherent in that occupation, and what innovations Matt might try next. Since Matt didn't need to make a profit from ranching, only enough money to convince the IRS that Whitaker Ranch was more than a hobby and a tax write-off, he could branch off into whatever areas interested him. His ranch hands did all the work while he dreamed up new enterprises to pursue.

Tony was interested in Jordan's veterinary practice. He specifically asked how a town of less than a thousand could support the clinic.

Kat noticed that Jordan didn't take offense at the question. She knew he understood that Tony wanted to be certain that his sister was in a stable relationship.

"If I was dependent upon the town's population, my business would indeed be struggling. But I'm the only large animal vet for fifty miles. The clinic only exists as a convenience for the locals. I support myself from billing rich ranchers like Matt."

"That's the truth," Matt piped up. "My vet bills top twenty thousand dollars a year, and I get the family discount. Do you have any idea what he charged me to vaccinate two hundred goats?"

Kat jumped into the conversation. "Whatever that amount was, it wasn't large enough."

Everybody at the table laughed.

"The clinic supports itself, more or less,"

Jordan said. "Torrey is better qualified than I am to tell you if we break even. The clinic doesn't support me, however. In addition to my ranch customers, I board strays. The county supervisors find that cheaper than building and maintaining their own animal shelter."

Jordan continued talking about his practice. "I also do consulting for the U. S. Forest Service. They have their own animal and plant management agency, but when they need a vet on site, I'm here and familiar with the local conditions."

Kat jumped in again. "Being a high-country vet, Tony, is a lot more than just giving puppies and kittens vaccinations."

"And you like this work?" Tony asked.

"I love it," she replied.

"Even taking a horse's temperature?" Matt teased.

Kat grinned. "Even that."

Tony, picking up that he was missing some kind of inside joke, looked at Kat and asked, "How do you take a horse's temperature?"

"Very carefully," she said. "And beyond that, you don't want to know."

The table erupted in laughter again.

Kat got up from the table and started

removing dinner plates and the remaining food. Torrey joined her, and soon they made short work of clearing away the debris of the meal. Kat sent Torrey to take orders for dessert while she brewed coffee.

When coffee and pie had been served, the conversation settled to the hum of contented people. They all complimented Consuela's pecan and pumpkin treats. Matt promised to carry their words of appreciation back to his housekeeper.

After Kat checked the kitchen to make certain there were no temptations for naughty kitties, she let the kids out of their prison. Calamity Jane scolded them loudly for their unfeeling behavior. Meanwhile, Brando headed directly for the dining room with the hope of pursuing his second favorite pastime, eating. But there were no snacks lying around for little kitties.

The men returned to the living room and the TV with the intention of catching the end of the Cowboys game. Kat and Torrey set about washing the china and stemware by hand. A companionable silence existed in the kitchen when Jordan walked in searching for a beer for Jeremy.

"I don't know where he puts all that food," Jordan remarked.

Torrey laughed, "He's still growing, you know."

"Seriously, Torrey, he's a full-grown man. The only way he can grow now is sideways."

"No chance of that," she replied. "He's too active."

Jordan suddenly became serious. "Active? What in the hell does he do? Anytime I ask him about his work, he just shrugs my questions off. One day he's here, the next he's gone. But he always has money. I hope to God he's not involved in something illegal."

"He's not," Torrey answered. "He just wants to live his life in his own way without his big brother or big sister commenting or criticizing."

"Torrey, are you telling me that you know what he's doing?"

"I have a pretty good idea, but it's not my place to say. Leave him alone and he'll tell you when he's ready."

TWENTY-ONE

Jordan was almost afraid of the happiness that Kat brought into his life. He couldn't imagine what he had done to deserve her, but he'd do nothing to cause her to retreat.

Holding her tightly, he thought back to her buying spree and decided that if buying items for the apartment made her happy, she could spend as much money as she liked. It wasn't as if she was spending cash on herself. She didn't buy fur coats or diamond bracelets. Her commitment to making their life more comfortable did much to assure him that she was here to stay—that she wouldn't abandon him as his mother had.

When there was a tap on the door and Jeremy wandered in, Jordan wasn't too surprised. His brother had impeccable timing.

"Did I catch you two noodling again?"

"Noodling, what kind of word is that?" Kat asked, laughing.

"The word is just something I read in an English Lit class a century ago, meaning embracing and kissing. I think it's from the same era as bundling, which meant sleeping together with all your clothes on so no serious sex could happen."

"Jeremy, you are a wealth of unexpected information—but enough of you showing off. Why are you here?"

"I've come to beg lunch—a sandwich made from my brother's finely roasted turkey."

Jordan laughed. "You are a mooch, little brother. But your flattery will get you fed if Kat is willing."

"Of course I'm willing. Your sandwich, however, might not be exactly what you anticipate. My *day-after* presentation includes cranberry relish and dressing as well as turkey. The concoction is messy, but oh-so-good. Are you game?"

"Bring it on, little sister."

Jordan raised his eyebrows at his brother's endearment, but he held his tongue. He was well aware that if he made of point of calling Jeremy out on his use of the *little sister* greeting he would only prolong the practice—something best not done.

Kat shooed Jordan and Jeremy to seats at the kitchen table. Then, she laid out all the ingredients on the counter and began assembling the sandwiches. She hummed under her breath while she worked. Jordan watched her with a heart full of love. When he recognized what he was feeling, he was dismayed. He hadn't any plans for their relationship to go so far. He'd no intention of falling in love. And he certainly wasn't going to get married.

Jeremy looked across the table at him and spoke in a whisper, "From the look on your face, I think you have just discovered what the rest of us have known for awhile. You're in love with Kat. What do you plan to do about it?"

Jordan started to claim his brother was wrong, but then accepted the wasted effort. As a result of being abandoned by their mother, the three siblings were bound in a way almost as closely as twins.

Keeping his voice as quiet as Jeremy's, Jordan replied, "Nothing. I'm going to do nothing. If I love her and she loves me, then I would be required to consider a permanent partnership.

That will never happen—the pain would be too great when the relationship ended."

Jeremy started to rebut Jordan's argument when Kat approached the table with lunch. "What are you two whispering about?"

"We were talking about what Jordan should get you for a Christmas present," Jeremy replied with a sincere look on his face.

Jordan had never realized what an accomplished liar his brother was. But at that moment, he was very grateful for Jeremy's ability to prevaricate.

Kat looked at Jordan. "Are we going to exchange gifts at Christmas, Jordan?"

"I thought we might," he said, barely able to squeeze the words from his mouth.

"What would you like?" she asked him.

Recognizing that his brother hadn't yet recovered his balance, Jeremy jumped in again. "He remarked that his lab coats are getting shabby. You could always get him some new ones."

"Jeremy, are you out of your mind? I am not giving Jordan lab coats for Christmas, or anything else for the clinic. That's ludicrous."

Jordan had recovered enough to laugh and enter the conversation. "My brother is pulling your leg. He has no idea what I want for Christmas. We were discussing gifts for you. We can talk in private once Jeremy has filled his stomach and moved on."

"But, bro, I like being here and stirring the pot."

"Jeremy, you and I are also going to have a discussion in private, but not right now. So eat, enjoy your sandwich, compliment Kat on her culinary skills, and then leave."

Jordan silently breathed a sigh of relief that the conversation had turned to subjects safer than love and permanent relationships.

The three of them focused on eating. Jordan wasn't surprised when Calamity Jane and Brando wandered into the kitchen following the scent of turkey. The kittens produced a welcome diversion. Kat begged to be allowed to feed the kids little bits of turkey. Against his better judgment, Jordan relented.

"Don't hand-feed them from the table. Wait until you've finished eating then fix them a plate and scrape turkey into their cat dishes. We will never again have a peaceful meal if they're hand fed, or if we immediately respond to their entreaties."

"Yes, Jordan," Kat responded meekly, but she

was grinning from ear to ear.

Jordan knew that Kat was about as meek as a Bengal tiger.

After shooing his brother out of the apartment, cleaning up the kitchen, and giving the kittens their snack, Jordan again encircled Kat with his arms. "What do you say we give that *bundling* thing a try?" he whispered in her ear.

"Dr. Jordan Walker, are you trying to lure me into bed?"

"Am I succeeding?"

"Only if you lock the door. I wouldn't be surprised if your brother came barging in again."

"Good idea," he said. And after throwing the dead bolt, he took Kat by the hand and led her into the bedroom.

TWENTY-TWO

Late Saturday morning, Bridget Morelli telephoned her daughter. Kat was relieved Jordan was down in the clinic preparing a supply order. She didn't want to have this conversation with her mother within his hearing.

Of course, Tony had told his parents about the developments in their relationship. Kat had never expected that he would keep the information to himself, so she wasn't at all surprised. She knew how her father would react—not well. But she was uncertain about her mother. After all, Bridget had encouraged her to manipulate Jordan.

Her mother didn't beat around the bush; she came right out and asked Kat if Tony's report was true. Was Kat sleeping with Jordan?

"Yes, Mom, Tony told you the truth. Jordan and I are lovers. We told him as much on Thanksgiving Day."

"Oh, perhaps I shouldn't have encouraged you the way I did." Bridget sighed into the phone.

Kat laughed. "I didn't seduce Jordan. We reached a mutual conclusion that we felt something for each other, and we decided to explore those feelings. I didn't jump into his bed, or at least not in a sexual way, the first time he told me he was attracted to me. We moved slowly, getting to know each other. When the time was right, we started sleeping together."

"Are you going to be married?"

"I don't know, Mom. We haven't talked about marriage. Jordan has a lot of baggage from his childhood. He may never be ready for marriage."

Kat heard Jordan's footsteps on the stairs. "Mom, I have to go. Jordan is coming, and I don't want him to hear me."

"I understand. Call me when you can. Bye."

Kat heard her mother hang up the receiver at the same time Jordan stepped through the door.

"Who were you talking to on the phone?" he asked.

"My mom called to wish us a Happy

Thanksgiving," Kat responded.

"You mean that Tony told her we were sleeping together and she called to see if what he said was true." Jordan lifted her chin and looked her in the eye.

Kat was embarrassed. She knew she was a terrible liar, which was why she didn't usually make an attempt to deceive people, especially Jordan.

"Everything is okay, sweetheart. You don't need to tell me what she said. Obviously, she loves you and is concerned for your wellbeing. I wish my mother had been as dedicated."

Kat moved into his embrace. "Jordan, I'm sorry. I just didn't want to talk about her call."

"Hush, everything is okay—or it will be if you'll fix lunch." He grinned, showing Kat all was good.

With an immediate change in her demeanor, Kat said, "What is the problem with the men in your family? You, Jeremy, and Matt are always hungry."

"Not always," he said with a shrug. "Just three times a day, like clockwork."

"Would you like some of the turkey and vegetable soup that we had last night, maybe with a salad and sourdough bread?"

Kat glanced out the window to the parking area behind the clinic. "Jordan, guess what? Matt and Jeremy just drove up." She sighed.

"They both have impeccable timing with regard to food," Jordan said with a laugh. "I'll set the dining room table for four."

The cats, hearing the noises they associated with goodies, wandered into the kitchen at the same time Jordan's brother and brother-in-law came through the door from the outside. Between the cats' meows and the men's greetings, the cacophony of sound was overpowering.

"Out!" Kat shoved at the men. "Go into the living room and take the kids with you. I'll call you when lunch is ready."

Knowing when not to argue, the three large men allowed themselves to be pushed into the next room by a little red-haired pixie. The cats followed with significantly less deference.

When Kat entered to announce lunch, she found Brando curled up in Jeremy's lap and Matt entertaining Jane with a ball of paper.

Jordan swept Calamity Jane up into his arms and told Jeremy to follow with Brando. After the cats were securely confined in the laundry room, the four sat down once again to eat together.

"Seems to me," Jordan said, "that you two are

spending an inordinate amount of time here. Why is that?"

"Kat's to blame," Jeremy replied.

"Me, how so?" Kat asked.

"I miss my wife," Matt answered. "She's been gone for nine months. I like being around Jordan when you're here because you give me a sense of family."

"And you, Jeremy, what's your excuse?"

"Basically, the same reason as Matt's. Being around Jordan is more comfortable since you came into his life. He's my brother and I like spending time with him, but he hasn't always been amicable. Now he is. Even when he's ragging on me, he taunts with brotherly affection."

"You think Kat has made that much of a change in me?" Jordan asked.

"She has," Jeremy replied, "and if you don't see that, you're blind. Don't let her get away, Jordan. The rest of us will abandon you forever if you do."

Jeremy froze. An icy silence descended on the room, before he found his voice again. "Jordan, I am so sorry. I misspoke. We will never abandon you. That was definitely the wrong word to use. I should have said we will be disappointed in you.

We love Kat, and we want you to keep her in your life."

He reached out to hug Jordan, trying to undo the pain he had inflicted.

Kat, recognizing this as a moment where she should not intrude, held her silence. Everything depended on how Jordan responded to Jeremy's plea.

Matt, too, said nothing. He kept his eyes focused on the soup bowl in front of him.

Kat could feel warmth flood the room when Jordan returned his brother's embrace.

"Not a problem, Jeremy. You've been putting your foot in your mouth since you first discovered you had toes."

TWENTY-THREE

The week after Thanksgiving flew by, and December rolled in on the tail of a snow storm. Jordan's thoughts were stormy, as well.

He had been thinking about his recent conversations with Jeremy, and had to admit that his brother was correct. Maybe he *was* in love with Kat. Without question, he would be a fool to let her get away. But marriage was too big a step. He had promised himself he would never allow a woman to hold his heart in her hands. No woman would have the power to do to him what his mother had done to his father.

How did Kat feel about him? Obviously she cared for him, or she would never have allowed their relationship to move forward to intimacy. She wasn't that kind of woman. She had come to his bed a virgin. Since she was willing to give him such an extraordinary gift, did she expect marriage in return? No, he didn't believe that she expected anything in return. She had given herself freely and without conditions attached. That was one of the reasons he thought he might be able to love her—she didn't have an agenda.

How did he feel when he thought of the possibility of her abandoning him? The idea was like a blow to his solar plexus, leaving him staggering and taking his breath away. He must bind Kat to him. He was selfish; he wouldn't let her get away. He wanted to make her happy, to assure her that she was the most important person in his life, and he wanted her as his partner and helpmate, but not as his wife.

He had no intention of fathering children who could be hurt in the same way he and his siblings had been. He knew his sister Jessica felt the same way about having children. He didn't know how Jeremy felt. They had never discussed it.

Feeling the necessity of being certain they were in agreement about their relationship, Jordan steered their conversation in that direction after supper one night. "We're living together as a couple, and I want to be certain I've not misled you," he told her.

"In what way?"

"You know I've no intention of getting married—not to you—not to anyone."

"Yes," Kat replied, "you've been abundantly clear about your intentions, or lack thereof. You and I certainly shouldn't even consider marriage. I've never dated or been close with anyone else. You're the first man I've slept with. I should have more experience before I think of entering into a permanent commitment with anyone, don't you agree?"

Jordan felt as if he had been slugged. Kat wanted to go on dates and sleep with other men?

"Kat, what are you saying? I thought you were happy in our relationship."

"Oh, I am . . . for the time being. And I've accepted your position on the subject of marriage. But eventually, I want a family. I don't believe in bringing children into the world unless they will be raised by committed parents—parents who are committed to each other as well as to the children."

"So you're already thinking of leaving me?" Jordan couldn't believe what he was hearing.

"Not any time soon, but I'll have to leave at some point," Kat said with a shrug. "You don't want a spouse and children—I do. Don't worry," she continued. "I'm not going to disappear without warning, as your mother did. You'll know before I leave, and I expect we'll keep in touch. I *would* like to stay in Spruce Creek. I like being here. But there is little prospective husband material in this town, so I'll most likely have to move on elsewhere."

Jordan was getting angry. "So I should just enjoy you while I have you and then let you go?"

"That's the way you want our relationship to be, isn't it?" Kat's tone was even and unruffled.

"Damn, Kat. I thought you felt strongly about us."

"I do feel strongly, Jordan. But I have no intention of trying to force something on you that you don't want. And why are you upset?"

"Because you're telling me that sometime in the future you're going to abandon me."

"No, Jordan, I'll not abandon you. Abandonment requires commitment and obligation. There is no commitment between us, and neither of us has any obligation to the other except honesty. And I'm being honest."

Jordan was frustrated. Kat made it clear that she accepted his desire not to marry, but she insisted that he allow her freedom to move on when she was ready. He wanted to be free from commitment, but he didn't want her to be. He knew there was no logic in his thinking.

Frustrated that he was unable to resolve the conundrum, he grumbled, "I'm going to bed," then stormed out and slammed the door behind him.

He stripped off his clothes and climbed between the sheets. Would Kat share his bed with him tonight, or would she sleep alone in her room? He was cold and he missed her, but he would be damned before he asked her to join him in his bed.

He should have known better. Kat couldn't be trusted any more than any other woman. She had stolen his heart and now she intended to break him into little pieces. He wished he'd never started the discussion. But he needed to be assured that she didn't have any expectations that he was unwilling to fulfill. His thoughts just kept going round and round in his head.

He willed himself to sleep, counting one every time he inhaled and two each time he exhaled. Eventually, he drifted off focused on counting and not on his pain. He woke once during the night to find Kat curled around him. He slipped back into oblivion, a smile on his lips.

KAT FORCED HERSELF TO WAIT until Jordan went to sleep before she followed him to bed. She was angry and hurt. And she had no intention of inviting more of his bitter rhetoric. It had been painful acknowledging that she understood his position only too clearly.

She hadn't lied to him. She had been brutally honest. She didn't want the future she had laid out in front of him. But she had no intention of pleading for him to marry her, especially when he was so adamant on the subject. She wasn't setting a deadline, exactly—she loved him too much for that. However, if Jordan didn't come to his senses and propose marriage she would move on—not soon—and certainly not until she had done everything in her power to bring him to heel.

Bridget hadn't raised a dummy. Kat knew Jordan carried a lot of baggage. She also knew he had to get beyond that baggage on his own. If he opened up to her, perhaps she could help. But she couldn't and wouldn't talk him into changing his mind, and she certainly wouldn't beg. She could only pray that he loved her enough to make that change himself. She believed he did, and that was the source of her hope.

Kat had been lucky to grow up in a cohesive family unit. She might complain about her parents and her brother, but she'd always known she was loved and wanted. She had an excellent example of strong womanhood in the person of her mother. Bridget never disagreed openly with Kat's father; she accepted any argument Emilio put forward on any topic with equanimity. But somehow her dad always came to the right conclusion, convinced he'd done so entirely on his own. She had years of observing her mother's behavior when her dad was being especially mulish. All she had to do was apply her mother's methods. She had taken the first step.

Jordan had been convinced that Kat would argue with him if she disagreed with something he said. The thought never occurred to him she would go along with his position just to let him come to his own conclusion that he was being pigheaded. She had never given him reason to believe otherwise. From the day they met, she had never hesitated to tell him when she thought he was wrong. But that was before she had fallen in love with him.

She didn't believe that she was being deceitful; she just felt she was taking the path of least resistance. She was under no obligation to argue with him. She thought she was simply giving him his own personal experience of *A Christmas Carol.*

He was being shown the specter of *Christmas-yet-to-come* without her in his life. But so was she, and that troubled her.

She made herself a cup of chamomile tea and settled in front of the fire, planning to savor the happy times she and Jordan had shared. In the days to come, that might be all she had to hold onto.

Brando mewed to be picked up, and she set him in her lap.

The two cats were as different as she and Jordan. Brando and Jordan both wanted their worlds undisturbed. They wanted their lives to sail forward without any waves, just a steady current, everything going their way. She and Jane, however, saw goals they wanted to achieve and went after them. They made waves. They stirred the pot. They caused their men grief. Such was the nature of women, yet men never figured that out. No wonder men claimed they could never understand them.

She tried to figure out what had started Jordan on his inquisition. Why now was he suddenly stressing his intention to remain single? She hadn't brought up the topic of marriage. Was he reacting to something Jeremy had said on Thanksgiving? But that was a week past, so again, why now? To her mind, it just proved that women didn't understand men any better than men understood women. Putting the unanswerable questions aside, she decided to get some sleep.

Kat moved through the apartment, locking up, putting away, and preparing for the night. She touched the treasured things she might be forced to leave behind. When she locked the door, she admired the changes she had made to their kitchen. She rinsed her cup, wiped down the counter tops, and pulled the red and yellow curtains closed, shutting out the night.

In the living room, she stirred the coals and put on a log to burn through the night. She made certain the fire screen was secure and that the kittens' bed was moved far enough away not to overheat. The little everyday rituals brought calm to her troubled mind.

She sifted the kittens' litter box and disposed of the waste. She thought how much she would miss Calamity Jane and Brando if she did depart. It would be as if she were leaving her children behind. Perhaps Jordan would let her take the cats. He didn't seem as attached to them as she was.

Kat went into her room and dressed for bed.

She thought about sleeping there, and then decided she was not going to deny herself the pleasure of Jordan's warm body just because he was in a snit.

When she opened his door, she could hear his steady breathing. She went to her usual side of the bed, only to find Jordan occupying her space. She smiled to herself as she realized he had migrated to her side because he was seeking her. So, she moved to the opposite side and climbed in, wrapping her arms about her man and holding him close.

TWENTY-FOUR

K at was still sleeping when Jordan slipped out of bed. He was relieved that she'd chosen to share his bed, even if she had waited until he was asleep to join him. He gave thought to waking her with hugs and kisses, and then decided against it. He wasn't certain how she would react. If she pushed him away, he would be crushed. She had the power to wound him as only his mother had.

He dressed quietly and went to the kitchen to make coffee. While the coffee was brewing, he dialed Jeremy's cell number. When his brother answered, Jordan said, "Where are you?"

"I'm across the street, camping out in Dad's old house. Why?"

"I'm bringing coffee; I need to talk to you."

Jordan poured coffee into two insulated travel

mugs, secured the lids, and left the apartment. He was glad he was wearing gloves and his parka. The temperature was well below freezing, probably below zero. He would need to move fast if he wanted the coffee still to be hot by the time he made it to his brother, even if he was only crossing the road.

Jeremy opened the door for him as soon as his feet hit the porch. "What's the problem, bro?" he asked as he led Jordan into the dingy living room.

A fire burned in the fireplace, keeping the temperature bearable. Even so, Jeremy wore a heavy ski sweater. Jordan couldn't imagine how his brother was surviving in the old place.

Pushing a mug into Jeremy's hand, Jordan blurted out, "Kat's going to leave me."

"Whoa, what did you do?" Jeremy asked as he motioned Jordan into an ugly overstuffed chair. There was no doubt in Jeremy's voice that Jordan was at fault.

Jordan explained that he had wanted to be certain Kat wasn't misinformed about his intentions. Then he told Jeremy the substance of their conversation the night before.

Jeremy sipped his coffee in silence. When Jordan got to the end of his story, Jeremy looked his brother in the eye. "Okay, if I understand correctly, she's not packing her bags and moving out today."

"No, but she will someday."

"Let me ask you this—did you honestly believe that she would stay with you until you both died of old age if you aren't prepared to give her a commitment and the children she obviously wants? That's not rational, and you are normally a rational person. If the circumstances were reversed, would you want to stay in such an ambiguous relationship?"

Jordan felt sheepish, but he spoke harshly. "Dad gave Mom commitment and children, and she still left."

"Jordan, you are as dumb as a bucket of hair. Kat is not Mom. She is everything I've been told our mother wasn't. She's honest. That's exactly what she was last night, painfully honest. She doesn't keep secrets, she's outspoken. She's loyal; she never speaks a word against you, though, as your brother, I'm confident she has cause. And she's a realist. She lives in the moment and accepts what life brings while always trying to put a bright spin on circumstances. She doesn't ask for what she knows she can't have."

Jordan stood and paced the room. He knew

his brother was right. "I don't know what to do. I can't live without her."

"It's not rocket science, Einstein. You marry her, of course."

"So I should go back to the apartment and propose?" Jordan asked in disbelief.

"No, you should not." Jeremy pushed his brother back into the chair. "You know, you certainly have been living like a monk. You don't understand anything about women at all."

"I admit that," Jordan said, nodding. "Do you mean to tell me that you *do* understand women?"

"No, I don't understand women. No man understands women. But I *have* acquired some knowledge that can be applied when dealing with the fairer sex."

Jeremy sat across from Jordan. Leaning forward, he said, "If you go back and immediately propose to Kat, she's going to be convinced that she has forced you into doing so. Two things happen. One, she decides you're a wimp, and that she can manipulate you into doing anything she wants. Secondly, she doesn't believe you genuinely want to marry her, but that you're just proposing to keep her from leaving."

"I hate to admit this, but she is doubtlessly right in both cases." Jordan sighed. "So what should I do?"

"First, we need to get this place habitable so that you and your bride can move in after the wedding."

"What's wrong with our apartment?"

"You won't want Kat going up and down those stairs when she's pregnant."

"Pregnant?" Jordan sputtered. "We're not even married yet, and you're talking about Kat getting pregnant?"

"Look at this from Kat's point of view. If you present her with the house, for the reason I just gave, she'll know you're serious about commitment and children."

"Okay," Jordan mused.

"I've been making minor repairs and doing some maintenance on this old place. I think the structure is fundamentally sound, but we should have Matt look it over to be sure. The wiring, plumbing, windows, and kitchen appliances need to be replaced. I think the roof is sound; I haven't had any leaks in spite of all the snow we've had. Matt is qualified to advise us, and has the connections to make those things happen. Ideally, you'll want the rehab to be well on the way to completion by Christmas, which is only three weeks away."

"Why Christmas?" Jordan asked.

"Because that's when you are going to propose."

Jeremy began to lay out the details of his plan.

KAT WAS FIXING BREAKFAST WHEN Jordan returned to the apartment. "Hi, where have you been?" she asked, handing him a cup of coffee and taking the two travel mugs from him.

"I was across the road talking with Jeremy. He's rehabilitating the old house where we grew up. I was unaware he was there. I guess I pay little attention to the lives of the people around me."

Kat bit back a barbed response and asked instead, "Your dad's old place?"

"Yeah, Jeremy is living there." Jordan told her about Jeremy's assessment of the building and that they would ask Matt for help.

"You might want to go there, Kat. You did such a great job brightening up the apartment— you could offer suggestions for paint colors and furnishings."

"You don't think Jeremy would feel I was intruding?"

"Not at all, I think he would welcome your input."

"I'll think about your suggestion, but meanwhile, come sit down and eat while breakfast is still warm."

They both acted as if the argument of the night before had never happened. Kat had believed breakfast would be stressful, but Jordan seemed perfectly relaxed. She was disappointed; she couldn't believe that she meant so little to him. Her statement that she would be leaving at some date in the future was like water off a duck's back.

Jordan thanked her for breakfast, gave her a kiss on the cheek, and started out the door on his way to the clinic. Just another normal day.

"Don't forget we're closing at noon today and giving the staff the afternoon off," Kat reminded him. She heard his acknowledgement as she closed the door behind him.

Men. How could he be so calm? Kat wanted to pound some emotion into him; she needed to burn off her frustration.

She called the clinic to tell Torrey that she had things to do in the apartment and to call her if her presence was required. When that was done, Kat rolled up her sleeves and decided on a top-to-bottom house cleaning.

She started in Jordan's den with furniture

polish and a soft rag. She buffed until the mahogany desk and credenza could be used as mirrors. She ran the vacuum with such force it almost inhaled the hand-woven Turkish carpet. When she was done, she closed the cats out and moved to the next theater of war.

The bathroom she left for Jordan. That was his job, as was mopping the hardwood floors.

In Jordan's room, she stripped the sheets off their shared bed. With just one bed in use, the laundry loads had been cut in half. Usually, because she was so small and the bed was so high, she and Jordan would change the sheets together. But today she got a step stool and attacked the project like a Ute brave on a rampage.

She was on a tear. She felt good working her irritation out with physical labor.

In the living room, she moved furniture—which was no small feat—to make space for a Christmas tree. Jordan didn't know it, but they were going to get a tree today. When she was growing up, her family always set up the tree the weekend after Thanksgiving. She was already a week late.

She'd like to call her mother and share her woes, but Kat feared her mother might point out that the contretemps were all her own fault. Besides which, her mother would be at school. Christmas break was two weeks away. She thought of phoning Tony. Then she reconsidered, because he'd become the protective big brother and blame everything on Jordan. She was being forced to work on their relationship by herself.

Well, then, she needed to make herself indispensable in Jordan's life. He normally cooked dinner, but it wasn't a law engraved in stone. She got out the bread maker and her starter to bake a loaf of sourdough. She rummaged in the freezer and refrigerator. Yep, she had all she needed to prepare homemade lasagna. Her grandmother Morelli's recipe was unsurpassed.

She chopped and thawed and mixed and browned. In no time, she had sauce cooking in the Crock Pot®. Her grandmother always praised the convenience of slow cookers.

Jordan didn't have a noodle press, but she could make lasagna noodles without one. The recipe was simple—flour, eggs and a pinch of salt.

Kat had mingled useful exercise to burn out her agitation and the nurture of fixing food to settle her soul. Not a bad combination, she thought.

Since she had done all she could toward dinner, Kat decided to go across the road and see if Jeremy was there. She let Torrey know where she would be, pulled on her coat, and headed out.

Jeremy must have heard her on the porch because before she could knock, he opened the door.

"I hope I'm not intruding."

"Of course not. Jordan told me he was going to suggest you come over and offer decorating tips. Matt is coming by this afternoon to talk about construction issues. I'm excited about making this place habitable again."

As he showed her around the house, Kat took the opportunity to quiz Jeremy about his childhood. Since he had never known his mother, he didn't have Jordan's level of hostility toward the woman. Jeremy talked freely about growing up without a mother.

"Torrey was always there. I never knew anything different, so I was content. But Jordan wasn't about to let Torrey replace our mother." Jeremy gave her a wan smile. "She could clothe and feed him, she could intervene with his teachers, but she wasn't his mother and he let everyone know that. In the beginning he was hateful to her, but eventually she earned his trust. But to this day, he has never trusted another woman. I hope, Kat, that you are successful in breaking that record. I do think he is happier since you've entered his life," Jeremy added.

"After the argument we had last night, I'm not certain I would agree."

"Do you want to talk about it?" Jeremy asked.

Jeremy wasn't her mother and he wasn't her brother, but Kat felt comfortable with him and trusted his good intentions. So, unaware he had already heard Jordan's take on the incident, she told him everything.

When she was finished, he made no comment. "Aren't you going to offer me advice, or tell me not to worry?"

"You don't need advice from me. And I can't tell you not to worry because I know just how stubborn and wrongheaded my brother can be. The only thing I will tell you is that I'm here if you want to talk."

Kat beamed at him. "Jeremy, thank you. Would you consider marrying me if Jordan doesn't? I honestly want to stay in Spruce Creek."

Since she was teasing, Jeremy answered her in a similar vein. "Wouldn't work. Jordan would run me out of town on a rail if I stole his girl."

Kat gave him a hug and went back to the apartment feeling better than she had all day.

WHEN JORDAN WALKED INTO THE apartment shortly after one o'clock that Friday afternoon, he smelled the aroma of Italian food that permeated the kitchen.

"What are you cooking?" he asked Kat.

"Dinner," she responded.

"You didn't come into the clinic today?"

"No, I called Torrey. She said everything was quiet. So I told her to call me if I was needed. Then I cleaned the apartment, baked bread, started dinner, and visited Jeremy."

"Wow, why all the industry?" Jordan asked.

"Because we're going to get a Christmas tree this afternoon and I wanted all the chores out of the way."

"Let's have lunch, and then we can get a tree," he agreed.

"Food—is that all that you ever think about?"

Jordan pulled Kat into his arms. "I regularly think of one other thing," he whispered. He was determined to act as if the fight the night before had never happened.

Laughing, she gently pushed him away and went into the kitchen to make sandwiches.

After they finished eating, Kat dragged Jordan out of the apartment to cut a Christmas tree. The two of them could've driven up to Matt's ranch. He'd be more than willing to let them take a spruce from his property. Or they could've gone to one of the Christmas tree lots. But instead Jordan drove west on a dirt road into the national forest. The Forest Service road was passable, just barely, but Jordan knew exactly where he intended to go. When they arrived, he pulled onto the berm.

He lifted Kat down from the truck and, taking her hand, led her into the forest. They were in an area that had suffered a fire fifty years earlier so the new growth was primarily aspen trees, but in some places the spruce had come back. Jordan led Kat to a small copse of the blue-tipped evergreens. They found a small one just over five feet.

After Jordan cut the Colorado Blue Spruce, they wrapped and tied the tree in a tarp he'd brought along, then dragged it to the road and secured it to the top of the SUV.

Kat was as excited as a child when they returned home. She was impatient when Jordan told her there were preparations to make before bringing the tree into the apartment. He built a wooden stand, leveled the bottom of the trunk, and only then did he nail the tree to the stand.

He had Kat lay a clean horse blanket on the hardwood floor in the living room. Atop that he placed a galvanized wash tub. Then he and Kat carried the tree up the stairs and into the apartment. After setting the tree in the tub, he added water.

"The water will help keep the tree fresh, and may discourage the cats from climbing," he said, "but don't count on it. Those two, especially Jane, can find innumerable ways to get into trouble."

The kittens were already circling the spruce, their noses twitching. Jane balanced on her back legs and swatted at a branch overhanging the floor. She wasn't quite tall enough to get a purchase.

While Kat put Christmas music on the CD player, Jordan went to retrieve the Christmas decorations he'd stored away.

Jeremy showed up, which wasn't a big surprise. "You're too early for dinner, but if you're hungry you can make yourself a sandwich," Kat told him.

"I can do that later," he responded. "But

actually I'd like to join you guys. I haven't decorated a Christmas tree since I was a kid."

"All of two years," Jordan teased. "Come along, then. Jump right in."

Jeremy grabbed a couple of ornaments and set to work. They argued good-naturedly about where the ornaments should be placed. They talked about their individual experiences as children decorating their family trees.

Jeremy said he had pleasant memories of decorating trees while their father was still alive. Torrey was always there with fresh-baked cookies and warm cocoa. Jeremy, as the youngest, would be held high by his father to place the star on the top of the tree.

Jordan shared the same memories, but not with the same satisfaction. He remembered feeling as if something or someone was missing. He always longed for his mother to come home, especially at Christmas.

Kat's were different, of course. She related that hers were also happy memories. She and Tony would each take half the tree and try to outdo each other in their artistry. Kat, as the youngest in her family, always placed the ornament on the top.

As they were nearing the end, Torrey arrived.

She brought fresh-baked chocolate chip cookies, still warm from the oven.

Kat slipped into the kitchen, telling her guests she was going to assemble the lasagna and put it into the oven. When she returned to the living room, Jeremy was seated on the couch with Brando in his lap. Calamity Jane was batting at one ornament that hung low enough for her to reach. Torrey and Jordan were seated in front of the fire talking quietly.

"You're both invited to stay for dinner. I'm making lasagna, which is in the oven now. Then we can have Torrey's cookies for dessert."

Jordan was glad she'd made the invitation. There was no chance that Jeremy would have left, but Jordan was pleased that Torrey would join them.

Kat settled onto the couch next to Jeremy, idly scratching Brando's head. "Hey, the tree isn't finished," she said looking up.

"What do you mean?" Torrey asked. "It looks lovely to me."

"The angel hasn't been put on. Jeremy, that's your job."

Jeremy looked taken aback. "Are you certain that you don't want to do it, since you did it when you lived at home?"

"Here you're still the youngest, so it's your privilege," Kat said with a smile.

"Not by much, Kat. You're only a few months older than me."

"Nonetheless, you're the youngest. It's tradition. You get the honor."

Jeremy glanced down at the cat in his lap. "But I'll disturb Brando."

"Brando will survive and be back in your lap the minute you sit down. Now, take the angel and place her on the top of the tree—please."

Jeremy, who often behaved as the family clown, solemnly picked up the Christmas angel and reverently put her in the place of honor.

Jordan sighed as he began building new and happy Christmas memories.

TWENTY-FIVE

After breakfast on Saturday morning, Jordan told Kat that he was driving to Denver. He just didn't tell her why.

When she offered to accompany him, he suggested instead that she should do her Christmas shopping on the internet. While she appeared disappointed, she didn't make an issue of his suggestion. Jordan breathed a sigh of relief because he hadn't known how he would discourage her had she pursued her offer.

Before leaving the apartment, Jordan slipped into the bedroom and pocketed Kat's favorite ring. If she missed the bauble while he was gone, he hoped she would think she'd left it in the clinic. She frequently removed the ring because it had an elevated stone, something he intended to keep in mind while shopping for an engagement ring.

The drive down the mountain was uneventful. The plows had cleared the pavement and piled the snow on the shoulders. The sun was shining overhead casting a cold clarity on every visible object. While bright, the sun held no warmth. Jordan estimated that the outside temperature was barely above freezing.

Initially he felt confident. Then, as he neared the jewelry store in Lakewood, Jordan began to doubt. What if Kat genuinely didn't want to marry him? What if she insisted she wanted to date other men—sleep with other men—before committing to a lifetime with one man? What if that man wasn't him? She had seemed so unconcerned about them staying together the night of the argument.

When he entered the store, he was almost ready to turn around and leave. But before he could make an escape, a saleswoman greeted him.

"Hi, I'm Leslie. How can I help you?"

Feeling he would be rude if, at that point, he ran out of the store, he gritted his teeth and returned her greeting, introducing himself.

"Let me guess, Jordan," she said with a warm smile. "You're looking for a special Christmas gift for your lady. Is that right?"

"Yes, but now I'm not sure."

"Why don't you tell me what you had in mind?"

"I thought I would give her an engagement ring for Christmas. But I'm not certain how she'll react."

"You haven't asked her yet, and you're afraid she'll say no."

"More or less."

"I suspect you're worrying over nothing, but in the event that the worst happens, you may return the ring for a full refund."

Jordan wasn't worried about money as much as having his heart handed to him on a platter. He didn't feel entirely convinced, but now was not the time to chicken out.

"She's very petite," he said. "And she works in a veterinary clinic, so I can't get her one of those high-pronged diamonds that perch on the top of the ring band."

"Do you know what size ring you need?" Leslie asked.

"I brought her favorite ring with me. I'm hoping she won't notice before I return."

"Very resourceful," the woman said with an approving nod as she took the ring that Jordan offered and slipped the band onto a ring-sizing stick. "Your lady wears a size six," she said as she noted the ring size on an order form.

"Now, let's find a ring that you like. I think we'd best go with a channel setting. The stones are placed side by side within a metal channel. The stones don't rest on top of the band."

She reached into the display case and offered a gorgeous ring with a cathedral princess cut diamond and channel-set side stones. "If this ring isn't satisfactory, we may need to go with a promise ring instead of an engagement ring. I'm certain we'll find something to suit."

Jordan took and admired the ring. "This ring is lovely. What is the difference between a promise ring and an engagement ring?"

"A promise ring is more modest. The stones are smaller, and they are far less expensive."

"No, I don't want a promise ring. Kat deserves the best I can afford. How much is this one?"

"The ring lists for just under thirteen hundred dollars. We offer a payment plan."

"No, a payment plan's not necessary. Do you have this ring in her size?" Suddenly Jordan had no hesitation. He knew what he wanted right now.

"I'm afraid not. All the rings we stock in the store are six and a half. I'm certain we can have one here for you before Christmas."

"I live and work in Spruce Creek, up U.S. 285, this side of Fairplay. Is there any way I could have the ring delivered to me before Christmas?"

"We could send it by special courier, but if we have a storm that closes the highway we might miss the deadline. Wait here while I see what I can do."

Leslie locked the display case and took the ring with her into a back room.

In less than five minutes, she returned. "I have good news. Because of your particular circumstances—that you live so far from Lakewood and can't easily return to pick up the ring—the jeweler will size the band now. You may take it with you."

"How long do I need to wait?"

"Not terribly long. Why don't we get the paperwork taken care of and then I'll check on the sizing progress."

She proceeded to write up the sales invoice including a complete description of the ring—size, diamond weight, and gold karat description. Leslie also encouraged Jordan to purchase insurance that would repair or replace the ring in the event either the stone or the band were damaged or lost.

Jordan gave her his credit card and the transaction was completed. She left him for the back room again and came back carrying the resized engagement ring.

"Let me have the ring you brought with you," she said. She slipped the band onto the sizing stick again. "Note where it rests," she instructed Jordan.

She removed Kat's ring and slipped the engagement ring onto the sizing stick. "Does this match the size of the other ring?"

Jordan agreed they did match. So he signed acknowledging he had received the merchandise and walked out of the jewelry store with Kat's engagement ring in his pocket.

SINCE JORDAN WOULD BE GONE all morning, Kat decided she would do her Christmas shopping online as he had suggested. In addition to his gift, she wanted to get gifts for Jeremy, Torrey, and Matt. She would, of course, also purchase Christmas presents for her parents and her brother and have those gift-wrapped and shipped direct.

First she needed ideas. Her mom and Tony would be easy to shop for. Her father, not so much. She had no idea what to get for her friends in Spruce Creek. She visited sites that promised ideas for gift giving.

She purchased an exquisite emerald green pashmina-and-silk shawl for her mother. Bridget would both love and wear the stole. She wondered if Torrey would like something similar. Kat kept the thought in the back of her mind while she continued to surf the net.

Who would believe that Christmas shopping this way could be so easy and so much fun? She got up to stretch and the cats came begging for a treat. After giving them some kitty nuggets, she returned to her search.

For Tony, she got a book on rock hounds in Colorado. He had a master's degree, and was working on the dissertation for his Doctorate in geological sciences, so the book wouldn't tell him anything he didn't already know but might provide a fun outlet for the use of his knowledge. She could easily picture him wandering through some rocky draw picking up stones to be polished.

Her dad did not lend himself to creative gifts. He wore a shirt and tie to work. He didn't have any real hobbies other than golf, so Kat was stymied. She could think of nothing special that he might like. Finally, she settled on fine leather gloves lined with cashmere. At least he would have warm hands.

Kat got up from the kitchen table where she had her laptop and walked into Jordan's den. She stood there waiting for inspiration. Nothing came to mind. She wanted something special for him, something he couldn't walk into the local gift shop and buy for himself.

The kids had followed her in and were snooping into corners and under furniture. They were rarely allowed in this room so, for Jane at least, this visit was an adventure. Kat only wished she had gotten as much satisfaction from visiting the den as the kittens did. Since magic hadn't touched her, she shooed them out and returned to surfing the web.

After much searching, Kat found marble bookends with the distinctive veterinary caduceus—a single serpent, no wings and a distinctive V—rendered in pewter. The bookends would definitely be a unique gift. Unlike a doctor's caduceus, which was relatively common, the veterinary symbol was much harder to find.

She would like to have the gift engraved, but

didn't because the site couldn't promise the bookends would be delivered in time for Christmas.

The hardest part was finished. For Matt and Jeremy, she didn't feel the need to be especially creative. So for Jeremy, she purchased a beer-making kit. Since he loved beer so much, she thought he would enjoy making his own. And because Matt spent so much time out in the cold, she decided on a goose down vest, tall and extra large. She just hoped the garment would be roomy enough. Matt was a big man. She would sign the gift cards as being from her and Jordan.

For Torrey, she selected a warm wool scarf with a bright tartan plaid. Kat had seen her wear a similar neck wrap on numerous cold mornings.

She paid for gift wrapping for her family's gifts and for rush delivery for everything. She felt confident that all the gifts would be under the tree before Christmas.

Kat was disappointed when Jordan returned home without any boxes or bags. She had assumed he'd gone to Denver to shop. Once again, she was wrong. She could never anticipate what he would do.

Of course, he was hungry when he came in. That condition she could always anticipate correctly. "Why didn't you eat while you were out?" she asked.

"I wanted to get back to you as soon as I was able. I missed you. And I like sharing my mealtime with you, better for my digestion."

"You are full of flattery, what's the occasion?"

"We're getting close to Christmas and I want something other than coal in my stocking."

Kat rolled her eyes, but smiled in spite of herself.

TWENTY-SIX

J ordan had been thinking about his recent conversations with Jeremy, and he had to admit that his brother was right on two counts. He was in love with Kat, and he would be a fool to let her get away. But marriage was such a big step that, again, he was having second thoughts.

But he had bought the engagement ring, and he began to imagine how he would propose. He wanted the event to be special and romantic. Something he could tell his children—about the night he proposed to their mother. *Children,* where had that thought come from? He hadn't asked her yet, she hadn't said yes, and already he was thinking about children.

When Torrey knocked on his office door and entered without waiting for his acknowledgment, he was sitting at his desk, still bemused.

Torrey looked at him, then looked around the office as if she thought he was hiding someone. "Have I interrupted something?"

"No, I was just thinking."

"Thinking, is that what you call what you were doing?" Then she changed the subject. "Do you remember that supply order I sent the first of last week?"

"Yes, of course." He hadn't a clue what supply order she was talking about, but it was better that she not know how little attention he had been paying to managing his practice lately.

"Well, the vendor is on the phone. He is out of the brand of antihistamine you ordered. He wants to know if you will wait or if you want an alternative."

"How long does he think it will be before they get the product from the manufacturer?"

"Maybe three weeks, possibly less." Torrey was still looking around the office, and then she looked back at him.

He wondered what she was seeing.

"I'll wait. We still have some on hand; I just don't want to run low at this time of year."

"Okay, I'll tell him. You can go back to your dreaming now."

After she closed the door behind her, Jordan realized Torrey was right. He had been dreaming—dreaming of creating a fairytale moment.

He wasn't allowed to go back to his reverie, however. The next person to knock on his door didn't wait to be invited to enter. Jordan groaned silently. The visitor was his least favorite cop.

"Detective Turner, what can I do for you?" Jordan stood and stretched out his hand.

The detective shook hands and said, "Dr. Walker, I think it's what I can do for you. Your brother's lead was solid. We arrested Roger Cassidy last night."

"How?"

"Jeremy told us where he was hanging out in Fairplay. We just needed to pop in from time to time until we caught up with him. You understand that we didn't have the manpower to stake out the bar, but we could make frequent visits anytime an officer was in the area."

"Are you going to be able to prove he is the one who broke in?"

"Don't need to. He confessed. He decided a nice warm jail cell is preferable to living on the streets of Fairplay during the middle of winter. Can't say as I blame him." Turner tried to get comfortable in Jordan's visitor chair. "Turns out he has a record for petty theft and misdemeanor assault—nothing major. This appears to be his first brush with B&E. He claims he didn't intend to hurt anyone. He was just in a hurry to get out and not get caught. So he ran over Miss Morelli."

"Ran over her? He slugged her with a flashlight. But I guess that should be no surprise. Any man who kicks a defenseless dog obviously is capable of braining a defenseless woman."

"Well, I wanted you to know that Miss Morelli is safe and can now move out of your apartment."

"I don't think so," Jordan muttered under his breath.

"Did you say something, Dr. Walker?"

"Nothing important, detective. I was just talking to myself. Thank you for coming by to tell me the good news. I'll let Kat know right away."

The two men shook hands again, and Turner left the office.

Jordan went in search of Kat to let her know that her clove-smoking assailant had been apprehended. He hoped she wouldn't grab on this as an excuse for her to relocate right out of their apartment. He was prepared to convince her that this was the wrong time of year to think of moving anywhere. She had just purchased items to spruce up the place.

He wanted a ring on her finger before she could even think about moving in that direction. If she brought it up when he told her the good news, he would tell her they shouldn't talk about it in the clinic but wait until they were together at dinner time. Then he would distract her.

At midday, Jordan met Jeremy at the house to survey what needed to be done before Jordan and Kat could move in. Matt Whitaker arrived at Jordan's invitation, and the three men set to work.

The house was over sixty years old—a two-story wood frame structure built in the 1950s. At that time, both land and building materials had been cheap. The exterior boasted a covered porch with a spindled railing. It was unclear if the porch was safe or not. The front yard was heavily overgrown.

The living room, dining room, kitchen, and master bedroom were on the ground floor, along with a den and a mudroom. The second story included four bedrooms and a playroom. There was only one bathroom on each level.

No one had ventured up to the second floor in years. Jeremy had lived frugally on the ground level. He slept in the master bedroom, cooked and ate in the kitchen—when he wasn't eating at Jordan's—and spent his leisure time in the den. He came and went through the kitchen. When Jordan asked why, he explained he wasn't certain he could find the front door key.

They all donned dust masks before beginning their inspection. The area Jeremy occupied was relatively clean and neat, but the rooms that had been closed off were deep in grime. Upholstery covers were draped over the furniture, but to even brush up against one was to set off a storm of dust motes flying through the air. As the three men walked though the house, Matt made lists of what the men could do and what should be done by professionals.

"The electrical will need to be replaced," Jordan observed. "Nineteen-fifty's wiring can't possibly provide for twenty-first century appliances. Matt, do you still own that contracting company in Denver?"

"I own it and I sit on the board of directors, but I'm not involved in the day-to-day management."

"Do you think you could scare up a qualified electrician to bring the wiring up to code?"

"I imagine I can do that, but you can't bring

anyone to work in this house until it's no longer a health hazard. The first thing you must do is hire a professional crew to clean the place out."

"Can you help with that?" Jordan asked.

"Can and will. I'll have a crew up here by next Monday. It will take a few days for a hazmat team to make this place safe enough for workers to come in."

"Hazmat, are you serious?" Jordan asked in dismay.

"Besides the dust and deteriorating fabrics, we have to be concerned with mold spores and the ever-prevalent radon found in Colorado soil. In addition to cleaning out the dust, the team will test for both those toxins."

"Jeremy, you're probably at risk even living in this house," Jordan said.

"Stop worrying. This is the first time I have been in this part of the house since I came back to Spruce Creek."

The men continued with their survey.

"I think we should focus on making the ground floor habitable—more than habitable, a homey environment," Jordan said. "The kitchen appliances will need to be replaced—they're all at least thirty years old." Looking at his brother he said, "I now understand why you eat at my place so often. It's a matter of survival. Okay, Matt, what do you have on your list?"

"You need the house thoroughly cleaned: carpets ripped up, window coverings removed, walls and floors washed. You need new wiring and plumbing hook-ups for a dishwasher and garbage disposal. I suggest having all the pipes in the house checked, water, sewage, and gas. You should have the windows replaced with double pane Low-E glass and vinyl-clad wood frames. Probably should have the insulation upgraded. All of these things should be done by professionals. I'll have my company line up crews to complete all this work. Don't worry; I'll give you the owner's brother-in-law discount." Matt grinned.

"What does that leave for us peons to do?" Jeremy asked.

"You, Jeremy, will get to patch walls, paint, and refinish the hardwood floors." Turning to his brother-in-law, Matt said, "Jordan, you have the hardest part, the purchasing. I know you don't want Kat directly involved in the refurbishing, but I don't think it would be wise to do any redecorating without consulting her."

"I wouldn't dare," Jordan admitted.

"Sounds like a plan to me," Matt said. "Do you mind if I go to the clinic to make those phone calls? Sometimes it's a pain not having phone service up at the ranch."

"No, come along," Jordan replied. "Then come up to the apartment for a late lunch. Jeremy, you're invited, too."

Both Matt and Jeremy declined. Jordan was surprised, but didn't press the issue.

On his way back to the apartment, Jordan decided he would let Kat know that he would be asking Jeremy to move into the apartment while work was being done on the house. He planned on inviting Jeremy to stay with them at the same time he asked him to be his best man. But he wanted to let Kat know in advance that he would be asking his brother to move in. He didn't think it would be a good idea to blindside her.

After lunch, Jordan coerced Kat into going across the road to the old house with him. As they came around the corner of the clinic they saw Matt's truck still parked in front of the house and the two men moving about on the second floor.

"Now I know why Jeremy's timing is always spot on. My brother can see through the windows of the apartment into the kitchen. He knows when we're getting ready for a meal."

"Well, that's one mystery solved," Kat said.

Jordan didn't knock before walking into the house. He called out as soon as they were through the door.

Jeremy called for them to come up to the second floor. Jordan handed Kat a dust mask, and donned one himself.

When they reached the second floor, Jeremy greeted Kat. "Just the person I want to see," he said.

Jordan thought about saying something to Jeremy about not having a greeting for his own brother, then let the thought pass. Matt greeted him, so Jordan didn't feel slighted.

Jeremy rushed on, talking to Kat. "We need a woman's input. Matt is going to get an electrician in to rewire the house. If this were going to be your house, where would you want outlets?"

"For starters, every bedroom should have two outlets on every wall. And there should be ceiling fans in every bedroom. Air conditioning isn't necessary at this altitude, but on summer days, second-floor rooms can get warm and stuffy."

Dragging her behind him, Jeremy pulled her into the bathroom. "What about in here, what would you do."

"Well, from a woman's point of view, this bathroom is impossible—too small, out of date, and non-functional. You don't need four bedrooms on this floor. Knock out a wall, take space from an adjacent bedroom, enlarge this bathroom and build a second one on this floor. Put skylights in each one as well as vent fans."

Jordan once again thought his brother was a genius. Jeremy was getting Kat to tell him exactly what she would want done to the house, without knowing the changes were going to be made for her. Matt was walking along behind them making notes and nodding encouragingly.

"How about windows?" Jeremy asked. "We plan on replacing them all with Low-E glass and vinyl-clad frames. What else should we do?"

"Make the windows as large as practical, let in lots of natural light," Kat said. "All the rooms should have the same standard size windows so that buying window coverings is simplified. And, of course, the windows should be operable with screens."

Even though she hadn't been asked, Kat continued on. "You should paint all the rooms a bright ivory or cream, soft but amplifying the natural light. If you desire an accent color, one wall in each room could be painted a pastel green or yellow or blue."

"What else?" Jeremy asked.

"Don't carpet the floors. The hardwood looks sound, so just buff and reseal."

"Wow," Jeremy said. "Kat, you're a dynamo."

Jordan watched as Kat blushed. "I guess I just got carried away," she said.

"Well, don't stop now, girl," Matt contributed. "We still have the downstairs to do."

As they all trooped down the stairs, Jordan whispered in her ear, "Great job. The lucky woman who gets to live here will appreciate your candid suggestions."

TWENTY-SEVEN

The last weeks before Christmas passed quietly. Jeremy was staying with them in the apartment while the renovations moved forward. But he went out of his way to be unobtrusive.

The progress on the house was impressive. Kat wasn't certain why the three men were pressing forward so insistently—she couldn't imagine why there was such a hurry to finish the project. But press they did.

Almost all the gifts Kat ordered had been delivered. The only items missing were Jordan's bookends. Each day she would rush to the front counter to see what Frank, the mailman, had brought. Each day she was disappointed.

Finally, on the Friday before Christmas, the long-awaited package arrived. Kat was relieved.

The clinic would be closed from noon through Monday. Frank didn't deliver their mail on Saturday if the clinic was closed.

Kat ran up to the apartment. When she entered, she locked the door. Jordan had a key, of course, but if he found the door locked it might delay him enough for her to get his gift out of sight. She pulled the gift wrap down from the top of a bookcase in the den, put there to keep the cats from strewing wrapping paper all over the apartment. Kat was convinced that raising children would never be as much trouble as parenting Calamity Jane.

She opened the carton to inspect the marble bookends. They had arrived intact and were of fine quality. She was pleased. Repackaging them, she stuffed the interior of the container with bright red tissue and wrapped the box in festive blue and silver Christmas gift paper and attached a big silver bow. Kat had just settled Jordan's gift out of sight under the tree behind packages for friends and family when she heard him at the door.

"Kat, let me in. I don't have my key."

She opened the door and pulled him into the warmth of the kitchen.

"Why was the door locked?" he asked

irritably, as he pushed into the kitchen.

"I'm sorry, Jordan. I was wrapping your Christmas gift and I didn't want you walking in on me. Torrey was supposed to call me when you told her you were headed this way."

"I didn't tell her. She was dealing with a vendor, and I had no intention of getting in the middle of that." He grimaced. "You know how I feel about vendors—a necessary evil."

"Okay, you're here now. Did you come up to eat?"

Pulling her close, his irritation disappeared as he asked sensually, "Umm, what's on the menu?"

"Jordan," she shrieked, "you're freezing."

"Well, then, you can warm me up."

"Stop behaving like a centaur, now's not the time. We'll have a bowl of hot soup, return to the clinic, lock the doors and let everybody go for the remainder of the day. Then we can come here and warm you up."

Jordan gave her a hang-dog expression, but acquiesced and pulled out a saucepan to warm the soup that Kat had made the day before.

She took the pan and shooed him into the living room with instructions to check on the cats and to stay out of his den, knowing full well that the den would then be the first place he'd go.

Since she'd already hidden his gift under the tree, she believed that forbidding him the den would keep him distracted.

The soup was just starting to simmer when he returned to the kitchen. "The cats are fine. I can't see that they've been into any trouble. And there's nothing in the den except for gift wrap, so why did you tell me to stay out?"

"Just keeping you from being underfoot while I'm putting lunch on the table," she said, scooping meaty vegetable beef soup into the new stoneware bowls she'd ordered before Thanksgiving. She handed them to Jordan to put on the bright red place mats.

When they finished lunch, Jordan went back down to work. Kat rinsed the dishes and then put away the gift wrap. When she was satisfied that everything was tidy, she followed Jordan down to the clinic.

When they were preparing to close, Mr. Gardner hurried into the clinic carrying Clementine in his arms. He rushed to the counter. "Please, Clementine needs help. She ate a Poinsettia my neighbor gave me. I don't think she's breathing."

Hearing the disturbance, Kat hastened into the Cat Pit. She gently took Clementine from the man's arms. "In spite of popular belief, Mr. Gardner, Poinsettias are not poisonous to cats. So that's not the cause of her distress." Kat could tell the pet was not breathing. She checked for a pulse and found none.

Kat thought quickly. She knew the man still harbored hard feelings against Jordan, so she decided to be the bearer of bad news. "Mr. Gardner, I'm sorry, but Clementine is gone. There is nothing any of us can do for her."

She thought he would collapse onto the floor, but he made it to a chair. He burst into tears and wept as if his heart was breaking—and it probably was, Kat thought.

Still holding Clementine's body, she sat in the chair next to him and let him cry himself out. When she spoke, her voice was warm with compassion. "We can take care of Clementine's earthly remains," she offered.

"No, I'll take her home and bury her near the catnip garden she loved to roll in. When spring comes I'll know she's close to me. But I don't know how I'll get through Christmas without her," he sobbed.

"Wait here, please," she instructed as she returned to the back work area still carrying Clementine's body.

"Jordan," she called.

He appeared immediately. "What do you have there?" he asked.

"Clementine has died and Mr. Gardner is inconsolable. What would you think of asking him to take care of the babies in the cattery over the four days we're closed?"

"If he would, then Torrey wouldn't have to take the kittens to her place and foster them. And it might divert him enough to salve some of the pain."

Kat wrapped Clementine's body in one of the special pet shrouds they kept just for these circumstances. Carrying the shroud-wrapped body, she returned to the waiting area. She knelt down next to Mr. Gardner. "I know this is a difficult time to ask a favor of you, but we have three small kittens that we can't leave in the cattery over the four days we're closed. Could you possibly foster them until the day after Christmas? We'll provide everything they need, if you'll provide a warm home and human attention. Can you do that, Mr. Gardner?"

"Yes, I can do that. If Clementine were still alive, I wouldn't. She never liked having other cats around. But now I can help the little tykes."

With a heavy heart, Kat left Torrey and

Jordan to close the clinic. She went up to the apartment with the intention of taking a shower and curling up in front of a fire.

TWENTY-EIGHT

Jordan was quiet when he entered the apartment. Thinking Kat might be napping, he went first into their bedroom. Not finding her there, he called for her. When he got no answer he went to find Jeremy, instead. Walking into his brother's room, he received the shock of this life. There was Kat, nude and disheveled in Jeremy's bed. Jeremy was holding her tenderly. Her head was on his shoulder and she clutched him for support.

"What in the hell is going on here?" he bellowed, blinded with rage. A knife thrust into his chest couldn't have hurt him more. "No, don't answer, it's obvious what's happening and I don't want to hear your lies."

"Jordan, it's not what it looks like," Jeremy

answered, standing up. "Calm down and I'll explain."

"I don't want explanations. Just get out—both of you. The two people I love most in the world, and you betray me." Jordan could feel his world crumbling.

"Jordan . . ." Kat pleaded.

"I should have listened to my instincts. You're just like every other woman. I don't know why I thought I could trust you." He almost spat the words. "Just get out. I don't want to find either of you here when I get back."

Jordan stomped from the apartment. *How could Jeremy betray him—his own brother? He knew what Kat meant to him. But Jeremy was dressed. Kat was the one lying nude in his brother's bed in his brother's room. She was obviously making good on her threat to sleep with other men. She was seducing Jeremy. He would forgive his brother in time, but he could never forgive Kat.*

Rushing away from the clinic, Jordan had no idea where he was going. He wanted to run away from the scene he'd just witnessed, but it was burned into his retinas. He couldn't talk about what he'd discovered—there was no one he could turn to. He couldn't bear the thought of admitting his humiliation and betrayal to anyone, but he wanted to vent his outrage.

He crossed the bridge over Spruce Creek and walked up the forest road he and Kat had taken when they had gone to find a Christmas tree. Then they had been so very happy.

Jordan sank onto a frosty rock. He wailed his outrage, emptying his lungs with a roar. Then he collapsed in tears. He felt the same agony he'd felt when his mother had rejected him.

He'd been there when she was packing to leave. He had begged her to take him with her. She had abandoned her entire family—husband and three children—but she had rejected him as well. They were abandoned. He was rejected *and* abandoned. That was his ugly secret.

Jordan didn't know how long he sat collapsed on the rock at the side of the road, but when he again became aware of his surroundings, his butt and the backs of his thighs were stinging from the cold. Exhausted by emotion, he heaved himself to his feet and trudged home.

The apartment was empty when he arrived.

SOBBING, KAT CLUTCHED JEREMY. "Why are we here like this? What happened?"

"Kat, you were zapped—an electric shock— then you fell and hit your head. Apparently you had just stepped out of the shower. Your heart stopped and I started CPR. I got a pulse but you still weren't breathing on your own, so I brought you in here to keep you warm and continue rescue breathing."

"I don't remember anything. Why were we embracing, why are we embracing now?"

"You were hanging between life and death. If I hadn't intervened, you'd be dead now. The reaction for us to grab each other and hold on tight is normal, gratitude for your survival. Had we been total strangers, we still would have done the same thing."

Releasing his grip on Kat, Jeremy stood and walked out of the room. When he returned he had a bath towel and a set of Kat's sweats. "Dry off, and put these clothes on. I'm going to take you by the medical center to be checked out."

After Jeremy left again, Kat stood shakily. Her ribs hurt, but she was able to dry off and struggle into the clothes. *Poor Jeremy, his bed was soaking wet. He would need to change his sheets. But then, he wouldn't be sleeping here, and neither would she. Jordan had thrown them both out.*

When they arrived at the medical center, Jeremy explained to the nurse receptionist that Kat had suffered an electric shock and lost consciousness. Kat just stood next to him shivering.

She was led into the small ER facility, had her sweats exchanged for a hospital gown, and was wrapped in warm blankets.

Scott Petersen was the physician on call. While he checked Kat out and treated the burn on her hand, he asked Jeremy probing questions. Where did the accident occur, had her heart stopped, did she stop breathing?

To Kat, Petersen sounded angry, as if Jeremy were somehow at fault. Kat couldn't take anymore of his verbal abuse. "Stop. Jeremy saved my life. He's not to blame for what happened."

"You're right, Miss Morelli. Whatever my dislike of Dr. Walker, I shouldn't take that out on his brother." He turned to Jeremy. "My apologies. Your fast action restarting her heart and her breathing did save her life. But you also cracked her ribs."

"I know," Jeremy responded.

"Where's Jordan?" Petersen asked.

"I don't know. He wasn't at home when the accident happened. He doesn't know Kat is here. But when he learns of it, I'm sure you'll hear from him."

"But I'll be gone by then," Kat said.

"I don't think so," Petersen said, shining a light into her eyes. "I must tape your ribs and I want to keep you here for observation in case you have another concussion from hitting your head. Since this accident is so close to your injury in September, you will stay here overnight."

"Tomorrow's Christmas Eve—you must let me go home."

"I'm sure I'll release you tomorrow, but tonight you stay here."

Jeremy spoke up. "Kat, with all that's happened, it's best you stay here. I'll make certain Jordan knows where you are and why."

Kat read the double meaning in Jeremy's statement and acquiesced.

TWENTY-NINE

Jordan had tossed and turned all night. His sleep had been interrupted by the recurring vision of a nude Kat wrapped in Jeremy's arms. Had anyone asked him last week, he would have said he trusted Kat implicitly, that she would never betray him. But he'd seen the evidence with his own eyes.

What made this morning even worse was that he still wanted her. His bed was cold without her. He was cold without her. He wasn't prepared to face the day, but he knew he needed to get up. The cats were at the bedroom door and wanted to be fed.

So Jordan followed his morning ritual, fed the cats, showered, and made coffee. He didn't want any breakfast; he had no appetite. He had no idea what he would do with the day. All his plans had included Kat.

When the phone rang he knew it would be Jeremy. He hesitated briefly before answering.

"Good morning Jordan," he heard his brother say.

"There's nothing good about this morning, Jeremy. What do you want—my forgiveness?"

"There is nothing to forgive. I'm just calling to say goodbye before I hit the road. I'm leaving my truck in the clinic garage. I assume you won't mind. I'm just taking my bike."

"What about Kat? Are you taking her with you?" He prayed Jeremy's answer would be no. But even if it was, what difference would it make?

"Kat's in the hospital being treated for electric shock. You really should have the bathroom fixtures replaced with GFI switches. If I'd not been in the apartment, Kat would be dead."

"Dead, what do you mean?"

"I mean, brother, her heart stopped beating, and she stopped breathing. The scene that you saw and so badly misinterpreted was Kat coming back to life after CPR and rescue breathing."

"But she was naked."

"Most people are when they step out of the shower. I was too busy saving her life to worry about her modesty."

"Why didn't you tell me?"

"I tried, but you refused to listen. You ordered us to leave, and then you stomped out of the apartment. You threw away the best thing in your entire life—Kat's love."

Now Jordan felt ten times worse than when he awoke. Had he destroyed his only chance at happiness? But surely Kat would forgive him—she was a warm, forgiving person.

"I'll call you the next time I'm in town," Jeremy said.

"Wait, Jeremy, don't go. Tomorrow's Christmas. You can't leave the day before Christmas."

"Why should I stay? Without a doubt, it will be the most miserable Christmas in the history of the dysfunctional Walker family."

"Stay because I need you, because you're family, because you'll forgive me for being so screwed up. Stay because we're brothers and I want you to stand up with me when I marry Kat."

"Whoa, do you really think Kat can forgive you for what you did to her? You're being uncharacteristically optimistic."

"She has to, Jeremy. I can't live without her." Jordan experienced panic in a way he hadn't since the day his mother left.

WHEN JORDAN REACHED THE hospital, he was a mess. There was no nurse receptionist at her post, so he went in search of Kat, assuming she would be in one of the three hospital rooms in the clinic. But none of the rooms were occupied. Where could she be?

He wandered over to the medical offices side of the building where he ran into Petersen preparing to leave. "Where's Kat? Jeremy told me she was admitted last night."

"She was. I discharged her this morning, and she had someone come to take her home. I was surprised that it wasn't you. But Jeremy had told me you were gone, so I didn't think too much of it. She and the baby are both fine. So you needn't worry."

Jordan hadn't heard a single word after *baby*. He bit his lip to keep from exclaiming his surprise. Turning, he walked toward the exit.

"Oh, Walker . . ."

Jordan slowed.

"Merry Christmas," Petersen called to his retreating back.

KAT WAS SOBBING. "Torrey, I don't know what I'm going to do. I love Jordan so much, and I believed he was coming to love me. But now everything is over."

Kat had confessed to Torrey how Jordan had found her nude in Jeremy's bed. She had also described Jordan's outrage and his cruel words and how his accusation of betrayal had destroyed her.

"Hush, child, you're just emotional as a result of a serious shock. Give it time, and your mind and body will return to normal."

"Nothing is going to return to normal any time soon. I'm pregnant."

Kat watched emotions and thoughts broadcast on the features of Torrey's face. The office manager should never play high-stakes poker.

"Does Jordan know?"

"I only found out for sure last night. The doctor tested me when I told him I thought I might be. I was concerned about the baby. So no, Jordan doesn't know."

"When did you first suspect?"

"Last week I was ragging on Jeremy without any reason. When I apologized he told me not to worry, that he had lots of experience with his sister's PMS. I started thinking about my last period and realized it was before Jordan and I made love the first time—the only time we had unprotected sex."

Kat was so relieved when Torrey embraced her. "It only takes once, as you now know. That's why there are so many unplanned puppies and kittens."

Feeling somewhat more stable, Kat itemized her problems as she saw them.

Jordan had thrown her out of the apartment so she had nowhere to live. She was guilty of causing a serious rift between the two brothers. She suspected she no longer had a job. And even if Jordan hadn't fired her, she couldn't work in the clinic with him anymore. She was an unwed mother-to-be, and while that wasn't the disgrace it once had been, she knew her parents would once again find her lacking.

Kat felt as if her world had imploded. But she had no option except to pick herself up and move forward.

"I can start over again on the Western Slope. I should be able to find another job in Grand Junction. You'll provide me with a letter of recommendation, won't you, Torrey?"

"Of course I will, Kat. But don't worry about

that now. Get comfortable on the couch. Your ribs must hurt and you need to rest for the baby's sake."

IF KAT WASN'T IN THE HOSPITAL and if she wasn't with Jeremy, there was only one other place she could be.

As he stood knocking at Torrey's door, his heart was in his throat. He could only pray Kat would forgive him.

"Jordan Walker, you're not welcome here," his office manager snarled when she opened the door. "You've hurt that child enough, and you aren't going to do any more damage to her spirit."

"Torrey, this is between Kat and me." Gently pushing her aside, he strode into the living area.

He found Kat huddled on the couch, cringing as if she expected to be struck. What an idiot he'd been. She should never fear him. *Never.*

Sinking to his knees in front of her, he could see how red and tear-stained her eyes appeared. Gripping her hand so she couldn't pull away, he met her gaze. "Kat, can you ever forgive me for being such a fool? I love you so much, I can't live without you."

"I forgive you, Jordan. But I can't forget.

Things can't return to what they were before. You don't trust me. No relationship can exist on a foundation that lacks trust."

"I do trust you, Kat, and I'll prove it. I'll tell you the entire story of my mother's abandonment. I'll tell you what no one else ever knew—not my father, not my siblings, not Torrey. I'll tell you my ugly secret."

Jordan told her the entire story of their existence as a family of five. He told her of the things he learned later about the situation between his parents. And he told her how he had come upon his mother when she was preparing to leave.

"I was six. I came into her room and she was packing a suitcase. I knew that meant she was going on a trip. When I asked where she was going and when she would come home, she told me she was never going to come back."

He could see that Kat was listening closely to him.

"I begged her, Kat. I begged her to take me with her. She refused. She told me I would only be excess baggage. She didn't just abandon me, she rejected me. No one else knows that happened. I was ashamed that I asked to go with her, that I was willing to abandon the others if only she would take me with her. I'm still ashamed."

"Oh, Jordan." Kat sat up and pulled his head into her lap. "You have nothing to be ashamed of. You were six years old. She was your mother; of course you wanted to be with her."

Jordan breathed a sigh of relief. Kat understood. He trusted implicitly that she would never tell another soul what he had just confessed.

He pulled the ring from his pocket. Filled with love he had never hoped to experience he asked, "Kat will you marry me, be my wife, be my confidant, be the mother of my children?"

"I will gladly add wife to my duties. I'm already your confidant and the mother of your child."

Her eyes were shining when he slipped the ring onto her finger and whispered, "You're simply irresistible."

EPILOGUE

Christmas Eve one year later

C ooing sounds tumbled from the baby monitor. Jordan knew his daughter was awake upstairs in her crib. A flush of happiness invaded his body. There was no doubt that he loved this new female in his life. Who knew one little girl could bring so much joy to her father?

"Kat, I'll change Faith and bring her downstairs," he called to his wife as he jogged up the stairs. She was busy in the kitchen making final preparations for the arrival of their extended family.

"Hello, little one," he whispered as he picked up the baby and put her on the changing table. "I think you probably need a dry diaper. What do you think?"

Faith made little chirping sounds while her

father powdered her bottom and made her ready for her first Christmas Eve. He dressed her in red footed pajamas decorated with reindeer and sleighs and jolly fat elves.

He carried her down the stairs and put her into her activity center in front of the Christmas tree. She chortled at the blinking lights while, bouncing up and down, she shook her rattle happily. The thing he loved most about his daughter was that she had her mother's sunny personality.

"Merry Christmas, husband," Kat said, wrapping her arms around Jordan when she entered the room.

"Merry Christmas, wife," he whispered back before he kissed her.

But, as usual, their married bliss was soon interrupted by the intrusion of family. Jeremy was the first to arrive, having to merely walk over from the clinic apartment across the road.

"Merry Christmas, bro. Merry Christmas, Kat." He gave Jordan a hug and kissed Kat on the cheek.

Matt and Jessica had picked Torrey up and brought her with them. Jordan was pleased that his sister had returned from New York. They all engaged in a group hug.

Emilio and Bridget had driven to Colorado Springs and left their car at their son's condo. Tony had driven them all to Spruce Creek in his four-wheel drive. No one would be stranded for long because of bad weather.

"You and Jordan have turned this old house into a beautiful home," Bridget said, hugging her daughter.

"With a lot of help from all the others here," Kat responded.

Not to be left out, Calamity Jane and Brando wandered into the living room while Kat was serving drinks and snacks. Faith clapped with glee when she saw the two felines. Jordan knew his daughter would be chasing after then as soon as she could walk.

He surveyed his home—completely remodeled now—and his growing family. He was filled with sublime joy and wondered what he had ever done to deserve such happiness.

Watch for Jessica's story appearing in *Simply Provocative,* the next book in the Spruce Creek series, coming soon.

ABOUT THE AUTHOR

Sharon Burgess was born and raised in San Francisco. She grew up immersed in all the exciting culture of the City by the Bay. Her mother's legacy to her was a love of reading, and Sharon had her first library card before age five.

She wrote throughout her corporate career, but it was all boringly factual—staff reports, white papers, user manuals, advertising copy. In her leisure time she read across all genres—fantasy, science fiction, westerns, mystery books. But she didn't discover romance until she read her first Nora Roberts love story after her husband's death.

"While my husband lived, I didn't need to read romance," Sharon shares. "I had it in my life every day."

She is an active member of the California Writers Club Tri-Valley Branch and the San Francisco Area Chapter of the Romance Writers of America.

When she is not in front of her computer writing or editing, she is comfortably settled in her recliner with a cat in her lap and reading a romance novel.

Visit her website at www.SharonBurgess.com.